GANGLAND CARTEL 3

Romell Tukes

2

**Lock Down Publications and
Ca$h
Presents**

GANGLAND CARTEL 3

A Novel by *Romell Tukes*

Romell Tukes

Lock Down Publications
P.O. Box 944
Stockbridge, Ga 30281
www.lockdownpublications.com

Copyright 2021 Romell Tukes
Gangland Cartel 3

Lock Down Publications
Like our page on Facebook: Lock Down Publications
@
www.facebook.com/lockdownpublications.ldp
Cover design and layout by: **Dynasty Cover Me**
Book interior design by: **Shawn Walker**
Edited by: **Jill Alicea**

Stay Connected with Us!

Text **LOCKDOWN** to 22828 to stay up-to-date with new releases, sneak peaks, contests and more…

Thank you!

Submission Guideline.

Submit the first three chapters of your completed manuscript to ldpsubmissions@gmail.com, subject line: Your book's title. The manuscript must be in a .doc file and sent as an attachment. Document should be in Times New Roman, double spaced and in size 12 font. Also, provide your synopsis and full contact information. If sending multiple submissions, they must each be in a separate email.

Have a story but no way to send it electronically? You can still submit to LDP/Ca$h Presents. Send in the first three chapters, written or typed, of your completed manuscript to:

LDP: Submissions Dept
P.O. Box 944
Stockbridge, Ga 30281

DO NOT send original manuscript. Must be a duplicate.

Provide your synopsis and a cover letter containing your full contact information.

Thanks for considering LDP and Ca$h Presents.

Acknowledgments

First and foremost, I will always give praises to the Most High, Allah. Thanks to all my family for the support, love, and loyalty. Thanks to all the readers around the world. Y'all my biggest supporters and the main reason why I go so hard with my pen game. A nigga said I was the HOV of the pen game. I believe him. You will too! Shout out to Yonkers, Peeky, and New York as a whole. Moreno, a.k.a. Smoke Black, YB, Lingo, Styles P. Jadakiss, DMX, the hometown… My BK fam OG Chuck and Black knowledge, my BX homies, Melly, D-1, and Frellz… My NJ homies, Beast, Rugar, Nap, T-Burn, BG. Shout out to Little Rock-Murda… Shout LDP always. It's a pleasure to be a part of something real. Black Lives Matters. We as people are all stronger as one. Every life matters. I will continue to push this street lit shit out. I feel like Ali in his prime wit' the pen.

Romell Tukes

Prologue
Russia, Kursh

PYT woke up in a small dark cage, naked. She looked around the large cage to see two women with kids who were also naked and scared to death. She could hear that she was on a train somewhere, but where? She felt her private parts to make sure she hadn't been raped, and it was a blessing to find that she wasn't.

The last thing she remembered was Rugar leaving the condo to attend a meeting so he could reach out to the Africans to ask them to leave PYT alone.

She went to sleep and was awaked by Mr. Hubei from the China Cartel family. She thought he was there because he somehow found out she murdered Hagar, but that wasn't it. He told her it was personal and that he was doing it for someone else. Then he stuck her with a strong tranquilizer that subdued her and put her to sleep.

The two women, who looked no older than sixteen, were quiet as they both just stared at her, wondering where she was from.

PYT could tell both of the women were most likely Liberian, Guyanese, or Bissau-Guinean. Luckily, she spoke Guyanese-Creole, Amerindian, and Grioulo, so she asked them in all three languages what was going on. They just looked at her as if she was crazy.

"We speak English," one of them said. Both women were from Khartam, Suder, but they were raised in America so they either spoke English or Arabic, since they were Sunni Muslims.

"Good. Oh my God, what the fuck is going on? How do we get out of here? Why are we here?" PYT asked them, as if they knew.

"Shhh! Talk low or they will kill you. We don't really know where we are going because we all have separate destinations," one of them said.

"Wherever you're going, it's not good. We were kidnapped coming out of a mosque in Chicago. They even took our little sisters," one girl said, holding her one-year-old sister for dear life.

"Who will kill us if we talk loud?" PYT asked in a low-pitched voice.

"The same people who killed them," one of the girls said, pointing to the next cage over where there were over twenty dead bodies of babies and women.

"Fuck," PYT said, sitting down in fetal position with her head in her legs, exposing her phat pussy, trying not to cry. She knew this was karma from all the people she had killed with no remorse, but she was willing to accept her fate. The only person she could think about was Rugar.

"Pssst! Miss, here they come! Fake sleep or they will kill you," the thick girl said. She closed her eyes as soon as the door opened.

PYT did the same as she heard footsteps and voices from a distance getting closer.

She couldn't make out what they were saying or their language, but the woman's voice was very familiar. It took PYT a couple more seconds to figure out who the voice belonged to and when she did, it made her blood boil as tears rolled down her face and legs.

The voice belonged to her sister Za'alya. It was all adding up now. Her sister and a male talked in a Russian language, which she understood well.

"I want the pretty one sitting in the corner with the long hair. She has an amazing body. I know she can bring in a lot of money," the man said, talking about PYT.

"Mr. Ivanovich, she is off limits, but we have two minors and two babies – black, the way you like," Za'alya stated, showing her pretty smile.

"She looks very familiar. Tell her to stand up," Mr. Ivanovich stated.

"Mr. Ivanovich, there is no need for that. Now please, let's go to the next load," Za'alya stated. She was wearing her all-black tight leather catsuit that she loved.

"But I want those two and the babies on my tab, plus the ten from the other carload," Mr. Ivanovich stated.

"Okay, that's fourteen. Follow me," she said as he followed happily like a kid in a candy store.

***

PYT heard this and felt sad for the little girls and the babies because they were about to be sold into the sex slave trade. There was something about the man's name that jogged her memory, but she couldn't put her finger on it.

"Oh, shit. Mr. Ivanovich from the Russia Cartel Family," PYT said, remembering him now. She had no clue he was into the sex trade because it was against the oath of the Cartel Commission rule #6: no sex slave trades of any kind. Never. The ruling was death.

"You two are going to Russia with the kids. They're going to make you sell yourself and they will use the babies as ransom. What are your names? I promise when this is over, I'll come to get you both," PYT said as tears poured down the young girls' faces.

"Jolien and Amber," they said, knowing their young lives were over.

An hour later, six men came to get the two women and kids. PYT was so upset she could do nothing except fake sleep to save her own life.

The train made a stop at Moscow in Russia, then continued straight to Harare, Zimbabwe.

Chapter 1

Chitunguiviza, Zimbabwe
Two years later

The dark, cold underground room barely had working lights with no windows and bars on a gate. The room was the size of two prison cells with a concrete bed with a thin mattress and concrete walls and floors. There was a steel toilet and sink which PYT used to bathe in with dirty brown water and a small bookshelf. She received two books every week.

This had been PYT's home for the last two years since she had been kidnapped from her home in the States. The China Cartel kidnapped her and handed her over to King Omen, her father, a powerful man who was the king of Zimbabwe.

PYT looked the same even though she felt as if she was on death row. She got fed three meals a day. The food was bullshit - normally rice, beans, and some type of wild animal. She ate it because she had no choice.

She sat on her bed staring at the wall, something she did for hours at a time to gain peace of mind. Sometimes she would talk to herself, but nothing crazy where she would answer herself.

Every day she would work out for three hours doing cardio burpees, jumping jacks, push-ups, squats, sit-ups, and lunges to stay in shape and toned and war ready.

The guards and Za'alya would normally come by to fuck with her and tease her about being Americanized, but she never said a word to them. She was militant and ready to die. When the guards would tell her that King Omen wanted to know if she was ready to take her position within his Empire, she denied everything, so her punishment was that she had to

remain in her cage being treated like an animal or prisoner until she gave in.

At times she wondered if Rugar still thought about her or even remembered her. She figured he had already moved on with a new wife, kids, and a happy life. She told him when they first met years ago that she wasn't wifey material and she lived a dangerous lifestyle, and he still wanted to be a part of it.

PYT heard the steel door open. She knew it was dinner time. The food had come around the same time for two years. They were snooping at her, she thought as she grabbed her plastic spoon.

"Dinner, my sister. I'm bringing it personally," Za'alya said, now standing outside her room. "This room would be nice if you had some posters of Jay-Z or 2pac. He was my favorite." Za'alya was in a nice black dress with sandals showing her pretty dark feet. "You haven't said a word in two years, little bitch. I begged Father to let me kill you and get this shit over with, but he refused," she said in her Shon language because her English wasn't all that good. She spoke many languages, just like PYT and their father. "Here go your food. Enjoy it," Za'alya said as she hocked spit into her rice. Then she slid it under the bars.

PYT looked at the food then at her sister, wishing she was on the other side of the gate.

"Oh, I forgot. Happy birthday," she said, walking away. Her ass clapped with every step. She was phat with no stomach, a toned body, and flawless dark skin. She was beautiful for a dark-skinned bitch.

When the door closed, PYT flushed the rice that had spit on it and ate the beans and raw fish.

"Stupid bitch," PYT said, wondering how she forgot it was her birthday. She was twenty-six years old, but it didn't mean

anything to her if she wasn't home with her loved ones to celebrate with her.

PYT grabbed a book called *The Brothers Karamazov* by author Fyodor Dostoyevsky, a book about human passions, lusts, greed, love, jealousy, sorrow, hatred, and generosity.

***

La Habana, Cuba

Rugar stood in the middle of the living room of drug lord Rodriguez Jr.'s mansion. He and his family of three were hogtied in New York style.

Rodriguez Jr. was a heavy coke supplier in Cuba, Venezuela, and Nassau. He had been supplying the city of La Habana, Villa Clara, Isle de La Juventud, and Matanzas. Rugar had a meeting with Mr. Rodriguez three months ago informing him that his turfs were now off limits and that they belonged to him and his cartel. He took Rugar for a joker being young, black and an American. That was his downfall, putting him and his family in the situation they were in now.

"Can we talk about this, Mr. Rugar? Please. I will leave Cuba forever, me and my family," Mr. Rodriguez said, looking at his beautiful Venezuelan wife, who could be a model since she was so sexy. Then he looked towards his three daughters, none older than fourteen.

"Oh, now you want to talk, my friend? Y'all hear this shit?" Rugar asked his sixteen man team of guards. They had already killed eight of Rodriguez Jr.'s security team while the other two ran into the woods behind the house that led into the mountains.

"Papi, I don't want to die!" one of the little girls cried, making her father tear up while his wife yelled something to her husband in Spanish.

"What she just say?" Rugar asked one of his men, since they were all Cuban.

"She said, she told him to stop selling drugs out here and he should have been killed ya," the big men said, holding an AK-47. "You fucked up now," the big man said in Spanish to Rodriguez Jr.'s wife.

Her eyes widened. She did not know the gunmen were Spanish because they were all blacker than Rugar. In a certain part of Cuba, most of the Spanish people were very like Dominicans and Haitians.

"She's right."

Rugar blew her head off. Blood spilled on her husband and kids as they screamed.

"Please, not my kids!" the man cried out, regretting taking over his brother's drug trade.

"Sorry, but in this game, there is no room for mistakes," Rugar said, shooting him six times in his face. "Take out the rest," Rugar said, walking out on his way to a meeting with the legislative members of the NCHC. They wanted him to be a member of the National Assembly.

***

The ride to Havana was long and quiet. Rugar sat in the backseat reflecting on life, mainly about losing PYT. Her crazy disappearance left many bewildered and puzzled, especially him.

Every day he thought about the last kiss he shared with her in her condo the night he got back from his meeting that went downhill because nobody showed up. His guards downstairs

were all murdered in the lobby near the stairwell leading upstairs.

Once in the bedroom, all he saw was a messed up bed and no signs of a fight, no bloodstains, no shell casings…nothing. Rugar had so many enemies throughout the years that he couldn't pinpoint who had either killed her or kidnapped her.

Normally a kidnapper would reach out for ransom money, but obviously that wasn't the case because it had been two years. He hired all types of people in different countries with the help of the Cartel families to find her.

He had a new pill product that was taking over the globe. 100 pills was equal to 1 brick of coke, but it was rawer and purer, thanks to his scientist. One pill was ten grams of uncut pure coke. A person could turn that ten grams into thirty grams of good cut coke, but nobody would know it was cut. Street dealers had to cut the cut over four times just so a person wouldn't overdose, and the pills were cheap.

Rugar had a lot on his plate with PYT. He knew she was still out there, and he was going to find her.

Romell Tukes

Chapter 2
Montego Bay, Jamaica
Montego Bay Prison

Big C had just stepped outside of the prison fence, a day he been waiting to see for over twenty years. Big C had a life sentence in the States for drugs, but since the new laws stated inmates with life sentences for drugs had to be re-sentenced to twenty-five years, he was the first immigrant to be re-sentenced. After spending all of his federal time in the States, he was deported to Montego Bay immigrant prison for eighteen months.

Years ago, Big C lost his son Lil C and his wife Michelle to gang violence. This crushed him while he was doing time in Canaan Camp in Waymart, PA. He used to hear from inmates coming in, fresh off the New York streets, about the Blood and Crip war, and the only names he heard were Big Time, Rugar, and Lil C.

One of his cellmates was a Crip from Harlem. He had never met Lil C, but knew everything about him. When his son was killed along with his wife, the chapel called him down to his office to break the news to him and offer him a fucking phone call. Since he was a federal inmate, he couldn't attend his son's or wife's funeral.

Days after his son's death, anyone in the jail who was gangbanging had heard about the death of the New York east coast Crip leader. Big C's celly told him about the crazy beef with Lil C and Rugar and how it was rumored that Lil C killed Rugar and that Rugar's goons inflicted retaliation.

Big C used to sit back and listen to his young dumb celly tell it all. He had to ask him to read his paperwork. He talked so much ain't no telling if he told something on his case. Big C never told the young man Lil C was his son. He just played

it cool and acted like he just wanted to be in tune with the streets.

He spent most of his time lifting weights, reading self-help books, taking college courses, and working in the prison kitchen. He also spent hours throughout the day plotting revenge for his son's murder, but since Rugar was dead, there was only one person's name left on the list. His celly told him about a female named PYT who had taken over.

Today he was finally released. He wished he could spend this with his wife, but she was dead. Big C saw three green Range Rovers pull up in front of him. He already knew who it was - a man he hadn't seen in years. But he received money orders from him every month of his bid.

Big C had long dreads. He was 6'4". He was forty-two years old, but looked younger. He was built like a football player. He had light skin and hazel eyes.

"Good to see you, man. Get in," his father said from the backseat of the first Range.

Big C hopped in with a small bag with his wedding ring, jail ID, and some cash.

"Thank you for everything, Pop. You look good," Big C told his father, who was smoking a phat blunt of weed.

"Yeah, man, prison did you well. But we have business to attend to," said Shota, who ran the Jamaica Cartel family. He was the most dangerous man on the Island.

"I'm sure we do," Big C said, taking long puffs of the strong herb that made him cough and choke while Shota laughed.

"Give me the joint, baby lungs," Shota said. His long grey dreads hung to the car's floor and he rocked his Rastafarian hat for his religion.

The trucks drove to Port Antonio, Jamaica, where Shota planned to show his son the new product taking over Jamaica's drug trade.

Big C had caught his Fed case for selling keys in the States and trafficking coke from South America to North America for his father. He didn't want to really get back in the game, but at this point, he had no choice. Refusing to sell drugs for the Jamaica Cartel was like snitching to the cops. You were a dead man if you didn't comply, and Big C would be no different.

"I still want to find out who killed my son and wife," Big C said, never telling his father he had a person in mind responsible for their killing because he knew his pops was strictly about business and he wanted facts before he moved a finger. Shota didn't believe in love; only success.

"Everything will fall in place," Shota said, thinking about the new shipment of pills his cargo ship had just brought in hours ago.

Big C looked out the window to see farms with goats, banana trees, and clear beach water. Jamaica had mostly mountains with a narrow, discontinuous, coastal plain and a temperate interior that was tropical, hot, and humid.

***

Florida Federal Women's Prison

Naya sat in her cell looking out the window into the empty yard with the neatly-cut grass and race track where she spent most of her time.

The prison was on lockdown because they had a big race riot on the yard with the Blacks against the Mexicans and white girls, who were normally racist anyway. The riot was

over a white girl stealing stamps from a black girl's cell from Texas to get high off of dope because she was dope sick. Three women were stabbed to death on the yard and one woman was shot from the guard towers. She made it, but she was in critical condition in an outside hospital. The jail was locked down for three days with twenty-seven more to go because the FBI and warden had to investigate the murders and charge people. Then they had to ship a lot of inmates out - mainly everyone who was involved in the incident.

Luckily, Naya and her celly Cat were at work in the laundry area when shit popped off or they would have had to put in some like the blacks did on the yard.

"Naya, what time is it?" Cat asked, waking up above her on the top bunk.

"It's 3:32. You were asleep all day and you were snoring again" Naya said, laughing and standing up to uncover the vent because the AC was blowing hard hours ago, but now it was off.

The girls' cell was a 6 x 9 regular cell with prayer rugs covering the floor as carpet, photos of their family members on their bulletin boards, and two lockers filled with clothes, food, and hygiene. The light was so bright they had to cover it with a crown legal large envelope, giving the room a red light district setting. There were so many Islamic books and urban books it took up all the space under the bunk.

"I'ma go back to sleep. Wake me up at dinner, sister," Cat said, tired and exhausted from their two hour cardio workout in the cell earlier that day.

Every day, Naya thought about the disappearance of her sister, which still saddened and baffled her. It had been two years and there was still no word of her, no trace of her body, and no witnesses.

Naya's son Brandon was now thirteen years old. Since yesterday, he was in Miami with Romell, who was his stepdad and her husband. Naya felt it was a good idea to let Romell raise him after PYT disappeared because Rugar had to run the Cartel and the Empire and she knew how that lifestyle was. Romell was pleased to raise his stepson.

Naya really trusted him and their marriage was still at its peak. He was holding her down 100% and she loved him for that.

Mail slid under her door and she got up to pick up the three pieces of mail. One was for Cat. It was from her brother, who was in the army. He always sent his sister money and pics.

The other two letters were for her. One was from Romell. He wrote to her twice a week. The other letter was from the Supreme Court of New Jersey, which made her heart stop.

Naya chose to read Romell's letter first, as she always did. He was just telling her how good Brandon was doing in private school and how he was number one in the state for martial arts in his age bracket. He also told her how he came to visit the other day, but was turned around because the jail was locked down. She placed the letter under her thick mattress and looked at the letter from the courts.

Naya had been waiting sixteen months to hear back from the court since her direct appeal was shut down. She had placed a 2255 motion sixteen months ago and this was the reply she had been dreading since she had been sentenced.

"Cat, wake up," Naya said.

"It's dinner already?" Cat said with her groggy voice and sleepy face.

"No, look. The courts just responded to my motion."

"Oh shit, read it, open it," Cat said, sitting up and climbing off the bed.

"Damn, stinky breath, brush your teeth," Naya said, smelling her breath.

"Come on, Naya, read it," Cat said, excited for her celly.

Naya opened the letter. It stated her motion had been granted in the Supreme Court and she would be re-sentenced under a new bill due to her RICO 846 indictment.

She screamed so loud the whole block heard her. Naya had tears rolling down her face as tears hit the floor. She made a quick du'cue to Allah, thanking him for his blessing.

The women talked all night about her winning her appeal. Even the women in the vent heard what was going on and everybody was happy for her.

Chapter 3
Miami, FL

Pressure grabbed both of China's legs and slid inside China's wet, tight, and warm gushy pussy, going to work. Once he opened up her walls a little, he built up a steady rhythm. He threw her legs further back as he got deep in her pussy.

"Ummm, fuck me," she moaned, grabbing the sheets, fucking the bed up as sunlight lit the room.

Pressure pulled in and out. His dick had her cream all over it as he pounded her pussy senseless with every stroke.

Once they both came, China was ready to take control. She climbed on top, sliding on his dick as it easily went into her soaking wet pussy.

Pressure sucked on her big titties while holding her small waist. Her phat ass bounced up and down on his dick.

Soft moans escaped her mouth as her hormones were at an all-time high.

"I'm cummminggg!" she yelled, squirting all over his dick, thighs, and bed sheets. China was a squirter, especially on some good pipe, and Pressure was the man for it.

China wrapped her juicy lips around his dick and sucked it slowly, making love to it while sucking all the cum out of him until he tapped out.

After their morning sex, they were ready to start their day, which was two different worlds. China was a defense lawyer for a big name firm. She had been with them for two years. Pressure was a household name in the street.

"I'ma have to put in overtime today, babe, so I won't be home until 11 p.m.," China said, getting ready to take a shower so she could rush to work.

"A'ight. I should be here. I gotta go. Hit me when you get to work." Pressure put his AP watch on his left wrist and his diamond chain on his neck.

"Okay, give me a kiss." China felt his wet lips touch hers and then she went into the bathroom in her cotton robe.

Pressure left their Key West mansion, which was 4,714 square feet in a gated neighborhood filled with rich people, mainly white. Six bedrooms, four bathrooms, a pool house, greenhouse, four car garage, and eleven acres in the backyard connected to a lake.

The two shared this house alone. Pressure didn't even allow his security to guard his house or even know where he lived. Pressure left his home and hopped in his all sky blue Wraith, which was parked next to China's candy red Wraith. It was a gift for Christmas from him: matching Wraiths.

Business was at its peak for Pressure, thanks to his boss Romell and his new product: the coke pills. Pressure didn't sell the pills. Instead, he would cook up ten pills at a time and receive a half brick of amazing coke that could be cut ten times more. The last couple of years had been a blessing. He was in a good relationship with China, he had a big army, and even more money.

He was on his way to Lil Haiti to see Dewan about a situation. He briefly spoke to him on the phone in code last night, but he didn't really understand so he told him to wait until the morning. Thirty minutes later, he drove the Wraith through the violent streets of Lil Haiti to see Haitian flags everywhere.

Pressure pulled up to a small liquor store he owned and walked downstairs into the small warehouse to see six of his soldiers standing around a nigga with four dreads. They called it palm tree dreads in Miami.

"Who the fuck is this?" Pressure asked his crew. They all had their pistols out.

"This bitch nigga was trying to sell on our block four times, but come to find out the nigga was selling soap for crack and selling baking soda for raw coke," Southside said. The dim lights in the room shone off his gold grill as he spoke in Creole, a language Pressure was good at because he was half Haitian.

Pressure couldn't help but laugh because he had sold soap when he was ten years old.

"Bruh, but that's not the crazy part of why he's here. The homie started to fuck him up and one of them found this on him," Southside said in Creole, holding a wire with tape that was found on his chest.

Pressure was pissed as he got closer to the nigga with the swollen face.

"Who you work for?" Pressure asked.

"Miami sent me, bruh, to get close to y'all. They don't know who runs the operations over here. Please, man, I just started working on the force. Spare me. I have kids. This is just a day job," the man said.

Pressure snatched the fake dreads off his head. "This nigga is a cop. Y'all slipping. Southside, tighten this shit up. If a nigga ain't with the family under you or me, kill him." Pressure saw a blow torch and axe on the table.

"We got you," Southside stated.

"Hold him down and cover his mouth," Pressure said.

They did as he asked. The man started to scream until they placed his T-shirt in his mouth and wrapped a towel around his mouth.

Pressure grabbed the blow torch. He watched the powerful flames shoot out as he placed it on the man's stomach, melting the skin off as the torch killed him slowly. Pressure then took

the axe and chopped off his head. On the eighth swing at the neck, his head rolled on the floor like a bowling ball.

"Clean it up, and don't call me back down here for bullshit," Pressure saw small bloodstains on his Rag & Bone jeans and his Louis Vuitton spike sneakers with the red bottom.

**

North Miami

Romell stood on the sideline watching the martial art fight at the MMA Center of Miami. The place was packed as everybody came out to see the best fighters in the city of Miami.

Brandon, a.k.a. Lil Brazy, his stepson, was fighting a boy twice his size and two years older than him. He was thirteen years old. Brandon had to compete with fighters older and bigger because he was too advanced for his age bracket.

"Let's go, Brandon!" Romell shouted like a proud father. He considered him a son and he guarded him with his life and treated him like a prince.

Brandon did a front flip and a powerhouse kick, making his opponent stumble backwards, then he did a flying roundhouse kick straight to the other fighter's temple, kicking him clear out as the crowd shouted.

The referee tried to wake the kid up, but blood spilled out of his mouth onto the mat. Brandon stood there in his black robe, hoping he hadn't killed him. Seconds later, the kid woke up, unaware of what had just happened to him.

The referee lifted Brandon's hand in the air and then bowed, showing respect as the crowd went crazy again.

"I did it, Romell, did you see me?" Brandon asked, running to Romell.

"Of course! You did great. You were patient this time. I'm proud of you. Come on." Romell let Brandon grab his duffle bag and say bye to his friend and the little girlfriend he had.

Brandon was 5'9" with a little muscle, long braids that reached his lower back, and grayish eyes like his mom and aunt. He got into kickboxing and martial arts two years ago and it just came naturally to him. He was the youngest black belt in the United States. He practiced karate, Kendo, Mai Thai, Brazilian martial arts, and kung fu, which was his favorite, thanks to his teacher, who was a grandmaster fighter.

Once they were in the all-black Maybach, the personal chauffeur drove them through the beautiful Miami streets with two SUV trucks tailing them, protecting their boss.

"Where we going?" Brandon said, playing on his iPhone.

"Out to lunch, kid," Romell said, smiling.

"Why can't we just eat at home?" he asked,

"Why you gotta ask so many questions? And if you must know, young grasshopper, we are celebrating," Romell said.

"Celebrating my win? I thought you told me we don't celebrate anything as Muslims expect Ramadan?" Brandon asked, looking at him.

Last year, Brandon became a Muslim. He found that the religion his mom and Romell practiced was meaningful and truthful. He prayed five times a day, went to Jumah on Fridays, fasted, and he learned his deen every day. He had a study hour after he did his homework.

"Well, let's say this is a blessed time in our life, Brandon. Your mother wrote me today and I found out she won her appeal."

"What does that mean?" Brandon asked, confused, knowing nothing about the justice system.

"It means she's coming home any day," Romell said, holding his emotions.

"What? That can't be? My mommy? Are you serious?"

"Yep," Romell.

Brandon started to dance to the music playing in the speaker, making Romell laugh.

The two had a good lunch at the Waffle House. It was a favorite spot for both of them. They both had so many things in common, including the same birthday: February 10th.

Chapter 4
Harlem, New York

Rugar stood up at the head of the table at the Empire meeting, ready to start along with the four men in front of him: Bullet, Red Hat, Big Smokey, and Twin.

"Gentlemen, hope all is well. This has been a long journey for us all, and thank ya for remaining rock solid with the fam. For the last few months, I was unable to attend the meetings for many reasons, but we all know the main reason," Rugar said, thinking of PYT. "I want to thank all of you for your help, support, and the blood y'all spilled for this Empire. That's why we will forever be on top," Rugar stated as all four men nodded their heads.

"This is what we do, Blood," Big Smokey stated.

"Today I come to you with good news - maybe the best news, since the new product that's taking over the city streets all over the globe. Naya just heard word back from the courts granting her appeal so she can be home any day. I spoke to her last night," Rugar said.

Nobody could believe it.

"Yo, that's crazy, boy," Red Hat stated, happy to hear this.

"I know, bro. It was just a matter of time after I won my shit," Twin said, thinking back to two years ago when he had won his appeal and given back his life sentence.

"I know she wants the seat I'm now sitting in and to be honest, I think she deserves it. We all know mentally I'm not fully there 100% after what happened to my wife. It's a lot on me to run a Cartel and this Empire, and I know Naya is focused. She was the day one mastermind with the guidance of my brother Brazy - may his soul rest in peace," Rugar said.

"We know what's up and we're here with you, B. Never question that, son," Big Smokey said.

"I know, but I'ma give the Empire to Naya. I just want to see if anybody rejects my decision. I'll still have my seat, but she will be head of the family," Rugar said strongly, looking around for them to respond.

"Well, you know what's best for you, Blood. Whatever you want to do, I support you," Bullet said smoothly while taking a sip of water. Since he found out he had diabetes, he had been on some health shit.

"I'm with whatever you feel, homie," Red Hat said.

"As long as the money keeps flowing, Blood, I don't care if Martin Luther King takes the head of the table," Big Smokey said, making everyone laugh out loud. "Nah, but you doing right, skrap. You still young. Move around, find your wife, and handle your B.I.," Big Smokey said.

"I'm just going with the flow, big homie, but I think she will be a big asset to us right now," Twin said, leaning back in his chair.

"A'ight, so when she touch down, roll out the red carpet for her. The shipment will still be at its normal pick up in Jersey at the loading dock on Sundays at nine in the morning," Rugar stated as he stood to leave ending their meeting.

Since PYT had been gone, Rugar had been running the Empire and the Cartel. It was a lot on him, back and forth on his own G-5 jet to Cuba and the States. Having to get drugs to all twenty three Cartel families was hard enough, especially with the pill product, and of course the heroin he was supplying the families. He was happy Naya was on her way home so that he could dedicate more time to find out what the fuck happened to PYT.

Everybody in the Empire was doing well. Bullet had opened more businesses. Red Hat was networking big time in certain parts of the south with Glizzy. They had the south in a chokehold. Big Smokey was living life, making babies and

getting money. As for Twin, he had the whole state of Jersey under his control from Newark to Jersey City.

Life was too good, but they all knew that wouldn't last long and they were all ready for whatever came their way this time.

***

Bulawayo, Zimbabwe

Za'alya sat Indian style in the middle of her living room, floor, surrounded by candles and black African snakes. They were zig-zagging all through the living room as if they were hunting. Za'alya wore a black silk dress with her back exposed, showing her scarified tribal tattoos as she spoke to the devils she worshipped with her eyes closed and her hands in the sky.

After her offering to the devil, she stood up and gathered all twelve snakes. Two of them had double heads. The snakes brought her closer to her devil and demons. This worship was a tribal religion in Zimbabwe. Some called them 666 servants, or devil worshipers.

Once all the snakes were in their tanks, she went to take a shower and prepare for her mission tonight in Yaoundé, Cameroon.

Za'alya washed her smooth dark skin with African black sea soap. She was very curvy, thick, with a toned body, nice C-cup breasts, a phat dark pussy with big lips, long jet black hair, hazel eyes, white teeth, dimples, and long eyelashes. Her beauty was remarkable. One would never consider her being the best assassin in Africa.

Since Zeema had been back in Africa, Za'alya had been a little over the edge. She wanted to kill her so badly. She was

upset with her father for protecting that piece of shit. She knew Zeema was next to take over the family kingdom and she was after her. Her father explained that PYT's blood was sacred - at least until he gave up his kingly position on the throne.

She hurried and got dressed in her black cat suit and grabbed her weapons of choice: swords, star knifes, blades, and her good luck necklace, which was a snake done in black diamonds. Za'alya climbed in her outdoor jeep with no doors and drove through the wilderness and forest, on her way to Cameroon.

***

Yaoundé, Cameroon

Father Paul ran the Catholic Church. He was from France, but he committed some sins over there which made a lot of powerful people mad. He ran to Cameroon five years ago and opened a Catholic church, since Yaoundé had a big Catholic population. He was a white French man in his 50's who wore glasses and a suit all day with a Jesus cross.

"Now Venny, you committed a big sin, and to every sin there is a punishment, even for a ten-year-old boy such as yourself. Since this is your first time in my office, the punishment will only last five minutes. It may hurt, but you can't scream or tell a soul. This is strictly between me, you, and God or Jesus, do you understand?" Father Paul said, already getting aroused at what he was going to do to his next victim. The church ran a yearly retreat for kids to study religion and living as well as orphans.

"I promise to never steal a colored pencil again, sir, please!" The Greek kid had heard stories about the monster from other students.

"Now, now, now, Venny, take responsibility for your action," Father Paul said, now standing over him in his chair. "I want you to imagine you're sucking a piece of candy, Venny. This is the easy part," Father Paul said, pulling out his hard four inch dick and shoving it in the little kid's mouth. "Umm, there you go, suck it," he moaned as the kid sucked the dick with fear.

The door flew wide open, scaring the shit out of the priest, making him jump backwards. Normally he would lock the door, but he was so thirsty for this kid that he forgot.

"You nasty bitch!" Za'alya used her nine inch blade to slice his throat open, leaving blood squirting everywhere.

The kid sat there quiet, frozen, watching the whole scene unfold.

"Thank you. He's a monster," the kid said.

"You're going to grow up to be gay, so I'm doing you the favor," she said before stabbing him in his heart twice, killing him.

A powerful rich French man paid Za'alya to hurt Paul and kill him for a half a million. He paid her half up front and he was going to wire the rest.

Romell Tukes

Chapter 5
Miami, FL

Jalee stood over three of his workers in Overtown, a dangerous project they called the strip, which was known for their drug selling and murders. He wanted his workers to cut dope with masks and gloves on because the heroin was so strong they would normally catch contact and be high as a kite.

Since he had moved to the city two years ago with his wife Hosayni, things had been amazing. He was getting money, the same thing he was trying to do in D.C. until the crazy beef with his brothers and father against the Empire. With all his family members murdered, he was the last of a dying breed. Now at twenty years old, he was focused on one thing: money. He was different from his brothers and father because he was mainly about money and family.

When he moved to Miami, he was hustling eight balls and ounces while Hosayni found a job at a daycare center. A kid named Rock introduced Jalee to Pressure so he could cop a couple of keys, and ever since, Jalee had been up playing with at least sixty keys a week at the minimum. He was able to cop a nice mini mansion Coconut Grove, a nice section in Miami for the middle and upper class. He had a nice Benz coupe and he brought one for Hosayni so she could drive to school and get from point A to B.

"How much more we got, Ja? I gotta go across town," LL said, almost done breaking the last brick down.

"That's it right there, slim," Jalee said, tying his mid-length dreads in a ponytail.

He had a lot of clients throughout Dade County. His name was ringing bells, not to mention he had killed two other known drug dealers. They had tried to force him out of their city, but he wasn't going for that.

There were a lot of niggas getting money in the 305. Romell and Pressure were number one, then Southside's and Jalee's names could be mentioned in the top ten. Jalee heard a lot about the man they called the King of Miami, Romell. Shit was so real rappers had to check in with him when they entered his city, including Miami native Rick Ross.

"I'm out, make sure all that shit gets to them Cubans in li'l Havana this time. Peanut, you almost started a war last time," Jalee said. Two weeks ago, Peanut started them on 12 bricks on their 42 key drop off, but he miscounted, which led to a gun standoff with Peanut, the Haitians, and the Cubans.

"I got you, bruh-bruh. That was a fatal mistake," he said being honest because he couldn't count for shit. He had a fourth grade education.

Jalee left the trap house, which had two pitbulls in the front yard behind the gates. There were a couple of young kids in their teens on bikes skipping school to sell dope for name brand shoes and food on their dinner table because most of the parents were the users.

Jalee hopped in the Benz and dropped the top because it was 97 degrees and you could feel every bit of it. As he pulled off, the kids yelled that that's who they wanted to be like.

***

Dade County Community College

Hosayni was in her English 101 class, taking notes and listening to her professor give study notes for the finals coming up soon. Hosayni got her GED the previous year and now she was in college trying to get educated. Before she married Jalee, she didn't know how to read or write. Now she

couldn't stop. She never thought she would be anything more than a servant or housewife.

Life was perfect in her books. She was happily married, had a house, car, and money…it felt too real and it was almost as if she couldn't believe it.

Males would approach her every day, but she would respectfully decline, letting them know she was married. Most could tell by the huge rock on her finger. She was the baddest bitch in the school: nice, perfect body, with an ass that was now filling out something crazy. Nobody could tell that Hosayni was a trained killer with a body count under her belt, outdoing most men, including Wayne Perry or the Son of Sam.

When the class was over, she was free the rest of the day. Since she started school, she had stopped working at the daycare. Hosayni still had money from two years ago when Mohammed paid her to kill Murder and his bitch Cherry.

She missed Iman Mohammed. He had saved her life, and that was something she'd never forget. When she was sold into the sex trade by the ISIS terrorist group in her birthplace of Syria after they killed her father and brothers, Mohammed got her from a French man, using her as a maid. She never met her mother and she never thought about it.

"Hey Hosayni, did you get all those notes from English? I was so busy texting with my dumb-ass boyfriend who I caught cheating on me with the school quarterback. I knew they were on some freaky shit. Who is twenty years old and still having sleepovers? He begged me not to tell nobody, but fuck that! I took pictures when I caught him bent over taking it from the back in his dorm room. I'ma put that shit on social media. What you think? I think I should go get tested. I can't believe I was sucking his dick. Eww! I should have known something was up when he always wanted me to lick his ass," Miley said, walking with Hosayni into the parking lot.

"Miley, oh my God, please stop! I don't want to hear it" Hosayni shouted, grossed out.

"My bad. I thought you could handle it better than me," Miley said, shrugging her shoulders.

Miley was a rich white girl from Key West. She was skinny with blue eyes, medium-length blonde hair, a couple of small tattoos, and a flat chest. All she had were big pink pierced nipples.

"I will call you later and email you the notes. Please don't kill yourself," she told Miley as she climbed into her Benz while Miley got inside of her Audi R8 with the clear suicide doors.

"Okay, bye," Miley said, speeding off and blasting the *Full Moon* album by Chris Brown, ready to go home and pop some pills.

***

Pinar del Rio, Cuba

Boom! Boom! Boom! Boom! Boom! Boom!

Savannah was hitting the middle target in her gun range located in her backyard. She was eighty feet away, hitting the middle circle every time.

Now in her early twenties, Savannah was more mature and smarter. Since the murder of her mother Hagar at the hands of PYT, life had been a little lonely for her. She was still a virgin. She had a couple of random niggas she'd meet in a club to eat her out, but that was far as it went.

She tried to blackmail Rugar years ago by telling him she would go to the Cartel families and tell them his wife killed Hagar after their affair. Unfortunately, that blackmail didn't last too long because PYT was either dead somewhere or she

had simply disappeared for some reason Savannah couldn't even figure out. She had no choice but to leave him alone after that because she had nothing to blackmail him with without PYT around or alive. She had her own mansion with a ranch, farm, and training area for Rugar's army, who she still trained five days a week.

Sometimes she would go by Rugar's mansion to check on him, but he wouldn't say a word to her. The two hadn't talked since the disappearance of his wife.

There was no doubt that Savannah was in love with him still and yearned for him to take her virginity, but she couldn't get him to fold. She had photos all over her house of Rugar. Her guards found that odd, but they kept their thoughts to themselves.

Savannah was looking like her mother nowadays. Her body was banging. She was glowing, and she had a strong sex appeal that teased most men.

Lately she had been heavily into the club scene and partying. She got bored sitting at home using her vibrator to the thoughts of Rugar.

Savannah walked into her mansion, taking off her work boots and army training gear. She stripped down into her bra and panties while two young guards stared at her big phat ass and plump pussy poking out of her pink panties.

"I bet you would love me to suck that cum out your dick while he fucks my phat pussy from behind, oh yeah! But sorry, keep dreaming, loser. I love black dick, not pink or tan," Savannah said in Spanish as she walked off, leaving their dicks hard and mouths open wide.

Romell Tukes

Chapter 6
Shanghai, China

Hubei sat at his oak desk in his high rise office at the People's Bank of China. He owned several across China. Besides owning a chain of banks, Hubei was the leader of the China Cartel. He had been a part of the Cartel Commission for over twenty years.

He was going through some important business documents when a person came across his mind, making him pause while he leaned back in his recliner leather chair. Needing a drink, he walked over to his in house bar full of all types of foreign liquor made in China.

After pouring himself a coup of Louis Vuitton XVIII, his mind flashed back to PYT and the part he played in getting her kidnapped. He knew if the other Cartel families found out about his role in PYT's sudden disappearance, he and his whole bloodline would be wiped out.

A couple of weeks before PYT was kidnapped, Hubei was asleep in his castle, 6,172 square feet of real estate worth 24.7 million. Waking up from his sleep to use the bathroom, Hubei looked over to his left, hoping to see his beautiful wife Yong asleep, but she was nowhere in sight.

Hubei walked around the third floor of his house, looking for her, calling her name. He knew she couldn't be far. He went to his twelve-year-old daughter's room, knowing she was sound asleep with her TV on watching a kid show of some type, as she did every night.

"Yiyangjum!" He yelled his daughter's name out so loud it echoed throughout the house as he ran down the three story flight staircase.

"Hanari! Guengx!" he yelled for his guards, who never left his house.

When he made it to the living room he saw four dead security guards with their necks sliced open like pigs in a halal shop. When he saw his wife and daughter tied up on the couch with tape around their mouths, his heart stopped. The unfamiliar female looked at him with a bright smile.

"Please let my family go. You can have whatever you want. Please, just let them free. Take me," he said, making her laugh.

"Mr. Hubei, I'm sure you're unaware of who I am, but I'm Za'alya and my father is King Omen. We need your assistance in something – well, with someone, I should say," Za'alya said, pointing a long sharp sword with a bloody tip at his wife's neck.

Hubei had heard of King Omen. Word was he controlled the poppy plants and heroin drug trade in Africa.

"What can I do? Please, just let them go. I can assure you whatever you want done could be handled with a phone call," he said, watching the tears fall from his wife's and daughter's eyes as they struggled to breathe through their noses.

"My father wants PYT - his daughter. I know she is a part of the famous Cartel Commission, so you have a better chance of getting to her than me. So I need you to kidnap her and bring her to me at a reasonable time. Then you can have your family back. Deal or not?" Za'alya said with her fearless stare.

"Give me my family first. How do I know if I can trust you?" Hubei stated.

"I'm sorry, Bruce Lee, but I make the calls. You can accept my offer, or I can kill all three of you and find another Cartel member," she said honestly.

"Okay, it's a deal. Please don't harm my family," he said, not knowing he just made a deal with the devil in a black bodycon suit with a pretty face.

"That's more like it," she said, smiling.

"Where will my family be placed until I do as you please?" he asked, praying he was doing the right thing.

"They will be well taken care of in a secret location nearby. They will be safe," she said, standing them both up from the couch.

"How can I get in touch with you?" he asked as she escorted his wife and daughter out the front, where eight guards were dead throughout the long driveway.

"You don't. I'll be in touch with you. I'll be watching you closely, Mr. Hubei. Don't do nothing dumb, little man," Za'alya said before walking out of his house.

Hubei promised to kill her one day for violating his code of honor and home. She went against the code of the land and he vowed to make her pay for it.

After he kidnapped PYT and brought her to Za'alya's location of choice, he was given back his family, but Za'alya was gone in the wind after he and his goon picked up his wife and daughter from a coal plant in Changqing.

Thinking back to those events gave him a chill feeling. He prayed PYT was dead somewhere because if this was to backfire, he would be in deep shit.

Hubei sat back down and called Rugar to check his mindset and let him know he was on the hunt to find PYT. She was a likable woman in his country.

***

Chitungwiza, Zimbabwe

King Omen stood outside the cage with a crowd of men behind him shooting, yelling, and screaming, watching the two African men fight for their lives.

Cage fights in Chitungwiza were *fight until death* with your fist or weapons. This was King Omen's fun, watching his tribal men fight for their lives. He would always treat the last man standing to a feast in his home.

King Omen had been the biggest dope supplier in Africa for over thirty years. He had connections all across the globe with some powerful people. When he found out his daughter was a part of the Cartel Commission, he had to bring her back home. Kin Omen knew Jumbo, but the two never saw eye to eye. It was never a beef. Both men knew of each other, but stayed out of each other's lanes.

He refused to let his daughter be a part of any Cartel when she had a position there under him. With his daughter refusing her position, he felt very disrespected, so he tortured her by keeping her in a underground cell where he would torture and kill other tribal men.

Until she agreed to his demands, he planned to keep her underground. He didn't care if it was five or ten years from now. He knew how to break someone and he knew it was only a matter of time before Zeema would be crawling to his crazy demands to take over the family business and throne.

African men yelled in their Shara language, all shirtless, jumping up and down while one of the fighters got the other African fighter on the ground and started pounding his face like a gorilla on Donkey Kong.

King Omen rubbed his long gray beard, watching the fighter beat the set out of his opponent. Within sixty seconds, the man was dead. King Omen told the winner to follow him to his home for the lion feast with twenty of his goons.

Chapter 7
Florida, Women's Federal Prison

Naya stepped outside the prison gates to see an all-red Wraith with black rims sitting outside the gates.

Naya couldn't believe she was really free after close to five years behind the wall. When she won her appeal, her appeal lawyer handled all of her court issues so she wouldn't have to go to court in New Jersey. She was immediately released, and today was that big day.

She saw Romell hop out. He gave her a big hug and kiss that brought tears to her eyes. She never saw herself falling in love with another after Brazy. When he had the shootout with police and got murdered, her love for another nigga left with him. After meeting Romell, he changed her outlook on love and life, but what really made her fall for him was how, regardless of however much time she had, he remained by her side. Every visit he was there, every phone call he answered, every new book from Lockdown Publications he ordered for her, every new magazine that came out, he copped it for her. There was no question he was everything she wanted in a real man and he was about his bag. When she left him over 130 keys of coke and dope, Romell didn't fumble the ball. Within months after she blessed him, he took over the streets.

What really made her realize he was the one she wanted to die with was when he offered to take her son under his wing and raise him. Naya was overwhelmed. She knew it took a man to raise a man. With her son being out in the free world and her behind bars, she understood there was only so much she could do in a fifteen minute phone call.

"Baby, I'm so glad you're home. Let's get the fuck outta here," Romell said.

Naya saw inmates on the yard yelling and waving at her, mainly her old celly Cat and a group of Muslim women.

"When did you get this fly-ass shit, baller?" Naya stated, admiring the red Wraith that cost 1.2 million fresh out the lot.

"This joint for you, love. I got an all-black one," he said, passing her the keys.

"Damn, baby, you know my style. Straight East Coast, bitch," Naya stated, climbing in the driver's seat in her Fendi sweatsuit and high heels to match. She looked sexy and younger, as if she had never left the streets.

"Just don't crush the Wraith. There is no warranty on this shit, ma," he said, hopping in the passenger seat, praying she still knew how to drive.

"Where we off to, captain?" Naya said, pulling out of the lot smoothly, loving the smoothness as the luxury car glided down the street.

"Home to your house, where your son awaits you, my Queen," Romell said as he turned up the Donell Jones album. He was thinking how thick Naya looked in the sweatpants. There was no doubt in his mind she got twenty pounds thicker in all the right places. He had only fucked one time and she had some of the best pussy he ever had. He had a lot of bitches, but Naya had that stalk a bitch pussy.

The two were in their own thoughts as they drove down the expressway heading towards Key West. Romell lived eight blocks away from Pressure.

***

Key West, FL

Brandon, a.k.a. Lil Brazy, was placing flowers and welcome home banners everywhere as the guards helped the maids clean up and prepare dinner. Brandon's heart was

racing. He would go see his mom every weekend with Romell, but nothing was like her being home. He used to dream about this day for years, and now it was coming true. There would be days at his private school were they would have parent day and only Romell would show. When teachers inquired about his mother, Romell informed them she was in the army fighting for her country. There was only one black old nosy teacher who did the math and figured out she was either dead or in prison, but she never pressed the issue because she knew her limits.

As soon as Brandon was about to run upstairs, he heard the guards let someone inside. Thinking it was his mom, he flew to the door, only to see China in her work suit and Pressure in a Balmain jean outfit.

"Lil Brazy, come here," China said, hugging her nephew. She hadn't seen him in two weeks since he spent the night over at their house when Romell went out of town on business.

"You're going to break my neck, Aunty," Lil Brazy said as she let him go so he could fix his little tuxedo that she fucked up.

"You look clean, kid. I heard about your last win. Word was you knocked him clear out," Pressure said, proud of him. Pressure really liked him because he was a good kid - honor roll student, respectful, and very smart. But he saw something in his eyes that reminded him so much of himself. Maybe the street life had him burnt out.

"Yeah, it was something. But thanks for coming. My mommy should be here in ten minutes. My step-pop just texted me. I'ma go get my gift for her. Don't go too far," Brandon said, running off as if he was a very busy man, reminding them of Romell.

"I never saw him this happy," China said, walking into the living room, which had a peaches and cream setting. The

wallpaper and rug were a peach color. The couches were all creamy white. The curtains were Dolce and Gabbana peaches and cream. The fireplace sat in the wall under the flat screen 62 inch TV, giving the living room a cozy feeling.

The mansion was beautiful. It had glass doors, two pools, a large Jacuzzi, a full-sized basketball court, eight bedrooms, five bathrooms, basement, large backyard meant for parties, eight car garage, a library, office room, and an exercise room in the rear end of the house. Romell used the space wisely. There were four big boy four-wheelers in the front and three 450 dirt bikes. Romell and Brandon would go hit some dirt roads in their free time.

"Brandon, they're here!" China yelled.

The guards and maids lingered in the backyard, setting up the food on long tables under white tents. All the food was halal. That was all Romell and Brandon as well as Naya ate due to their strict Islamic religion.

"Here I go," he said, running downstairs. Word was the whole Empire was on their way as well as Rugar, but Miami rush hour was just like New York.

"Surprise! Welcome home!" Brandon, China, and Pressure yelled as Naya and Romell walked through the door.

Brandon jumped in his mom's arms as tears poured down both of their faces.

"Oh my God, this is amazing! China, you grew so much, girl," Naya said, looking at China and giving her a hug. "Pressure, nice to meet you. I heard so much about you. Thank you for looking out for Romell. Your loyalty for him is never overlooked," Naya said, hugging him lightly. Because he was Romell's family, he was her family.

"Likewise. Glad you are home. I had my little cousin Baby D looking out for you in there," Pressure said. His cousin used to tell him how Naya was running the joint.

"Oh shit, she good people. That's crazy because she always used to tell everyone on the yard that we had a lot more in common than I thought, and I guess she was right," Naya said, thinking of Baby D. She was serving four life sentences plus 307 years. She had caught a jail house murder for stabbing her celly to death for stealing two Ramen noodle soups out of her locker.

"Mommy, Mommy!" Brandon said, passing her a pink box.

"What's this?" she asked, looking at how handsome her son was. He looked just like his father and Uncle Rugar, but with her colorful eyes.

"Open it," Romell said, smiling to finally see joy on his wife's face.

Naya opened the box to see a Rolex watch. She had never seen so many diamonds in a watch in her life. It was shining bright.

"It's called a bust down, Mommy. I got one too," Brandon said, smiling.

She looked at Romell, who shrugged his shoulders

"I bet you do," she said.

"Read the back," Brandon said.

Naya looked at the back and read it aloud. " 'I love you more than the world itself, Mommy. Your favorite and only son.' Thank you, baby. I figured your brother would be here, but guess he——"

"He what? A little late. Welcome home, Sis," Rugar said, walking in with the Empire all behind him.

"Oh wow, this day can't get no better," Naya said, hugging everybody, feeling the love.

Everybody talked and got to know each other because most of the Empire crew had never met Romell, Pressure, or China. They just heard of them and the men's rep in the south.

"Anybody hungry? The food is ready," Romell said, leading everybody to the beautiful backyard with the clean cut fresh grass, palm trees, and a view of the ocean leading into the Bahamas.

Loud music was on the big speakers in the back. Everybody enjoyed themselves eating, catching up with Naya, networking, drinking, and building a new bond with their Miami connections. The night went amazingly well.

After everybody left and Brandon went to sleep, Romell and Naya made love for four hours without either one trying to take a break. Fresh home pussy was a different type of pussy. Romell could vouch for that.

Chapter 8
Zimbabwe

PYT was laying down in a fetal position on her thin mattress that was the length of a blanket folded in two. She was asleep. It was still early and dark outside, so breakfast wouldn't be for another hour or so.

There was a rattling sound that woke PYT up out of her deep sleep. It sounded like a child whispering closing in on her. PYT's vision became full as she opened her eyes all the way to see a Black Mamba snake one foot away from her. She wanted to jump up and scream so badly, but she was raised around these venomous reptiles.

Now face to face with the deadly snake, PYT stood her ground and stared into the snake's dark beady eyes. She knew if a person was to move, react, look nervous, or run, they would be lunchmeat. After a ten second stare down, the snake did a lap around her cell and exited through the bars as if it had never come in. There was a loud clap within feet away from her cell, which made her stand up. She already knew it had to be one of Za'alya's evil tricks.

"Princess Zeema, that was amazing. I must say you're the second person in forty years I've seen beat the Black Mamba," King Omen said, playing with the deadly snake in his muscular hands, which were rough and ashy.

PYT just stood there in silence, thinking how close she just came to losing her life at the hands of her own father.

"I'm going to tell you a little story, Zeema, that I never shared with a soul. I had a brother named Mubbo Muzorawa. He was a couple of years older than me. After my parents - your grandparents - were murdered by another tribe, he was next to take over our family business and royalty. Muzorawa didn't want to, Zeema. He even ran away to Botswana, where

me and my brother, who you killed, found him." He looked at PYT to see no facial expression. "Well, once we found him, we kidnapped him and brought him here to this same room you're in, Princess. After five years of refusing his position, this little beautiful snake right here killed him while he was taking a shit," King Omen said with a laugh that sent chills up her spine. "You know why I love snakes? Because they can see through souls to the hell fire gates. The only reason you're not dead right now is because the snake saw demons in your eyes. Evil can never hear evil. No matter how hard you try, you will always be a demon child. Anybody who has any percentage of our bloodline is cursed, Zeema. Maybe next time, you won't to be so lucky - like your mother was forty years ago," King Omen said, walking off and slamming the heavy doors behind him.

PYT leaned back on the cold cement wall, hating the name Zeema. She thought about what her father just told her and wished she had a way out of there. If not, she would be dead.

She remembered years ago when she was having cold sweat nightmares about her upbringing in Africa. Now everything was starting to come to light as to why she was having those nightmares. It was her demons.

Lying back down, she couldn't help but picture Rugar. Without him clouding her mind, she couldn't go to sleep

***

Miami, FL

It was 11 p.m. and Jalee was parked in the Wendy's drive thru restaurant in his Benz, waiting on his connect to arrive.

Jalee felt like he was on top. Everything was perfect: beautiful wife, money saved, and he had a small crew under his command.

Years after his father's, brother's, as well as his mother's deaths, it was still fresh on his mind. He vowed one day to go to New York and find whoever was responsible for his family's murders. The only name that rang in his thought process was PYT's.

Pressure pulled up in a forest green Lamborghini Huracán with tints. This was how niggas in Miami rode. If it wasn't dark or with big rims or a luxury foreign whip, then Dade County niggas wasn't doing it.

Jalee got out and Pressure got out of their whips and they embraced each other.

"Sorry I couldn't check you the other day, but I was at a get together," Pressure said, checking the peaceful environment because the Feds would be hiding in a nigga's bushes just to get a picture.

"It's cool, slim. Glad you could make it on short notice. Shit been booming. I appreciate everything you done for a nigga since I touched your town," Jalee said. He really had a solid bond with Pressure because he kept it real with him since day one.

"No problem, little homie, this shit all part of the game, dawg. But check game, bruh, I got the order at your trap. It just arrived less than seven minutes ago. I got the same shit I've been hitting the streets with for a while. It's coke pills, but 100 is one key. You can stretch it to three keys of some fire, cuz. I know you only fuck with dog food, but this just on the house," Pressure said, tossing him a large medicine bottle filled with pills.

"A'ight, I'ma see what up. But hold on real quick." Jalee ran to his car to get a Nike duffle bag full of cash, all blue faces.

"Let me get the fuck outta here. But my boss wants to meet you soon. I told him about your numbers and he's impressed so when it's time, just be ready," Pressure said, tossing the bag in his passenger seat.

"Good looking," Jalee said, not evening knowing Pressure had a connect. This whole time, he thought he was the plug.

Jalee drove to his trap to make sure his workers were busting the bricks down and not stealing. There were over a hundred keys in the living room stacked up like Legos. This always made Jalee smile.

He was unaware of the car tailing him to his little meeting with Pressure and now here at his trap. Hosayni was making sure he was safe. She always tailed him at a distance while he took care of business just in case shit got crazy. She had a tracker on his phone in his car. She was very overprotective of him. She trusted him, but still refused to let someone take the only love of her life away from her. Some would call her crazy and some would call her in love, but she didn't care.

She went home knowing he would be on his way home soon as always and she would play sleep as always there was something about his connect that rubbed her the wrong way but she looked over it she didn't ever know the man who wore flashing diamonds and sometimes rolled ten deep. She knew it was a fucked game and she understood a nigga could be a friend one day then an enemy the next day.

***

Jamaica, Port Kaiser

Shota and Big G sat in one of the hottest nightclubs in Port Kaiser. Reggae music blasted in the speakers. The party-goers were all on the dance floor dancing nasty, sweating, having the time of their lives.

Jamaica is a known source and destination country for children and adults subjected to sex trafficking and forced labor. Sex trafficking normally occurred around the Port Kaiser streets, night clubs, and resort area for tourists. Shota was against it. If he heard of a nigga pimping minors or kids, he would find them and kill them.

The club had a lot of weed smoke inside of it. This was Shota's type of scene. He was an old man, but he still moved like a young nigga. They were sitting in the back enjoying the scene with seven bitches surrounding them while Shota's guards blocked off the whole section.

Since Big C came out of prison, he had been fucking all types of bad bitches. Shota had nine women that lived with him as maids. They attended to his sexual needs and they were well-trained for war. All of the women were about twenty-five years old. He refused to be another R. Kelly.

Big C was drinking Jamaican Rum, which was his favorite drink, but since he came home, his big body couldn't hold liquor at all.

"I got something I want to talk to you about," Big C said as all the ladies went to dance. They were waiting to go back to Shota's mansion for the after party.

"Speak," Shota said, watching the women put on a show on the floor, bouncing ass everywhere, twerking, throwing their asses in a circle. Women were doing splits in boy shorts.

"I know who killed your grandson, and I hear he is a very powerful man in New York," Big C said as Shota now looked at his son with fire in his eyes.

"When was you going to tell me this? I would have been had his blood clot's head!" Shota said in his strong Jamaican accent, puffing on the joint between his crusty lips.

"I was waiting for the right time. I know you run a Cartel, and——"

"Family is before business. Who kill me grandbaby?" Shota asked seriously, ready to kill.

"A man named Rugar," Big C stated with pain.

"Hold on, brotha, who?" Shota asked again.

"Rugar. But I heard he was dead and his girl PYT was the one doing the killing. I believe she is the one who killed my son because he was killed by Lil C. He is the reason why my son is dead, him and whoever she is." Big C saw a nervous look on his father's face, something he never saw before.

"I'ma ask you one more time: are ya sure it was Rugar and PYT?" Shota asked.

"I'm 100% crisp, man, it was them," Big C said, feeling the effect from the alcohol.

"Fucking bloodclot!" Shota yelled, slamming his fist into the table, making Big C jump. He had never seen his pops lose his cool like this.

"What's wrong? You heard of him?" Big C asked.

"Rugar is alive, you fucking dummy, and PYT is missing or dead. They run the Cartel Commission. If we go after him or even breathe too hard around him, this shit can get deadly," Shota said, wondering why, out of all the people in the world to kill his grandson, it had to be one of the most powerful men in the underground society.

"I don't give a damn who he is. I want my son to rest in peace," Big C said with drunk tears.

"Me too, son, but this can lead to a war with some very powerful people. I don't think you understand, brotha, but I'm with you. I had to play a grandfather from a distance through

Michelle. He had a career, a promising future as a boxer, and he took that from us," Shota said, patting his son on his back, letting him know he was with him.

"I got a plan."

"No, son, let me do the planning. You just be ready to put in work. A man is his own worst thinker when he is emotional," Shota said.

"I understand," Big C said sadly.

"Enjoy the night," Shota said as the women came back to the table.

High off ecstasy, one of them pulled out Big C's dick out and started sucking it under the table until he came in her mouth.

Romell Tukes

Chapter 9
Artemisia, Cuba

Rugar sat at the head on the long table, which was the length of half of a football field. The Cartel meeting was being held outside in the backyard of one of Rugar's mansions with a beautiful view of the mountains. Every Cartel family head was present except PYT, who controlled the USA Cartel family. Everybody was silent, looking at Rugar to begin the meeting.

"Good evening, ladies and gentlemen. It's another blessed year. Thank you for coming out. I'ma start off by giving thanks to you all for helping expand the new pill product. It's become very successful thanks to you all," Rugar stated.

"We should be thanking you," Ms. Costilla from the Colombia Cartel said, smiling because she had been making millions off the new product. Her country had never seen a product so strong. She grew coca plants herself, but it wasn't near as good as Rugar's work.

"Yeah, Rugar, you've done a lot for this commission with so little time," Katie said, looking like a hooker in her tight dress with a long V cut down the middle, exposing her breasts and side boob.

"Thank you. This shit isn't easy. I don't have a clue how Jumbo did this shit so many years, but I salute him," Rugar said, laughing, making everyone else chuckle as well.

"I'm still on the hunt for my wife. Her disappearance is still fresh to me. I believe she is still alive. I can feel it in my heart. I want to thank you all for the help and support, all the calls from Mr. Hubei and Juda. I appreciate the love," Rugar stated as Hubei nodded his head with a nervous smile.

Katie from the UK Cartel Family ice grilled Hubei. As long as she knew him, he was all for self. She found his

generosity to be odd, but she overlooked it and paid attention to the bossman.

"This year I plan to achieve a lot more new business aspects with the Pakistan and the Philippine families to produce petroleum pipelines so we can all have our hands in some oil. I also have a plan to establish something with the Djibouti family so we can also have our hands in potential geothermal power and some gold, but we all know the Djibouti Cartel family won't give a baby a hug," Rugar said as everybody laughed, including Mr. Smail, who looked more Ethiopian than Djiboutian.

Rugar talked for another thirty minutes, then the meeting ended. Everybody ate a big meal with all kinds of different foods.

***

All the families were leaving, on their way to either catch a flight or hop back on their G5 jets, which most of them owned.

"Rugar, that was good. I love the way you can bring all of us, man. Trust me, brotha, we all had our fair share of problems amongst each other, but when it comes to money, we all come togetha," Shota said, approaching Rugar in a black suit with a crown hat on, holding his long dreads in place.

"I'm glad I can be the one to do it, because we all bring something special to the table." Rugar looked at Shota. His small, evil eyes always looked sneaky.

"Crisp, crisp, me have a lot of respect for the youngsta in charge. But do you eva visit home? This place is like isolation," Shota said, looking at all the land, grass, trees, and mountains surrounding the mansion.

"I feel you. But since my wife disappeared, I just been somewhat in my own world. Shota, I can't lie, brother, I feel lost. When I do get time, I go see my nephew in Key West or visit my family gravesites. That's my only peace of mind," Rugar said, being honest and open, something he barely did.

"Live your life. Don't waste it under a rock. You're a good man," Shota said in his Jamaican accent as he left Rugar staring into the sky

Rugar thought Shota was an honorable man. Speaking to him just now made him respect his thought process a little more.

***

Atlanta, the Bluff

Glizzy was posted up in his hood trapping out of a fiend's house, chilling outside with his goons.

"Aye Glizzy, what's shawty name from Magic City with the butterfly on her ass with the bomb-ass head that be making nigga's toes cramp?" Mayo said in his loud voice, talking to a crew of niggas smoking, counting money, and serving fiends. They came back to back for the best crack and dope in the city.

"Man, you talking about Lexxy the Redbone," Glizzy said, hanging up from his phone call with Red Hat, who was blocks away.

"Yeah, yeah, yeah. Shawty stole 1200 dollars, my AP watch, and all my clothes. You know a nigga had on all designer shit. I'ma split that bitch's wig when I see her. That bitch better hope I don't kill her." Mayo stood 4'11" on his toes, but was known for busting his gun

"Mayo, you ain't going do shit. That was the same thing you said about Kimmy and Rolex the Body when they robbed

you and you still fucking them bitches, nigga," Rollo said, making everybody laugh except Mayo.

Down here, niggas talked to each other crazy. That was how they joked. But Glizzy was from New York. Calling a nigga a bitch was dying words.

"Mayo, I told you about tricking on them Magic City and Blo Flame hoes. I wouldn't be surprised if you got some shit you can't get rid of," Glizzy said.

"Shit, they told me they get tested once a month."

"Nigga, and I know you fuck them hoes raw, dog," Rollo said, puffing on some loud.

"So?" Mayo said. "It's my dick, nigga, I ain't fucking you," he said as the police rode by, paying them no attention because Glizzy had them on a payroll.

An all-white Ghost Rolls Royce pulled up to the curb and everybody watched Glizzy walk off.

"Damn, he riding clean as shit, folk," Rollo told one of the young niggas sitting on the stairs.

Glizzy walked up to the curb and out from under the shade, feeling the Atlanta heat that was always 90 and up in the middle of February. The only thing snowing in Atlanta was Glizzy's coke because since the BMF niggas got locked up, he had taken over the streets.

"Get in, Blood, take a ride with me, son," Red Hat said as he rolled down the window. Yasmine and Lyric got out in short booty shorts with ass hanging out the bottom.

"Damn...them bitches bad!" Mayo shouted as everybody agreed, shaking their heads imagining what they would do to them Spanish bitches.

Glizzy hopped in the back after he yelled to one of his workers to hold down the block as Yasmine and Lyric climbed in the front and they pulled off slowly.

Red Hat had a nice condo in Atlanta in the downtown area. Whenever he wanted to get away from New York he would pull up and fuck with Glizzy who had the city on lock.

"What's popping, five?" Glizzy said, dapping him up, happy to see him.

"Us, Blood; we popping. But I came to deliver news to you. Rugar stepped down and gave the Empire position to Naya. She just came home off her appeal. We all want you to be a part of the Empire," Red Hat said.

Glizzy looked shocked. This was his dream. "You serious, Blood?" Glizzy asked, happy as Michael Jackson in a day care full of little boys.

"You deserve it, bro. You been grinding hard out here. You built your own Empire. We need you and your family. So what you say?"

"Hell yeah!" Glizzy said.

Red Hat passed him a diamond five point star necklace, AP watch, and keys to a condo in New York and a Maybach, so he could ride in style.

"Thanks, brotty," Glizzy said.

They rode through the streets of Atlanta behind the Ghost, talking about future plans for the newest member of the Empire.

Romell Tukes

Chapter 10
Zimbabwe, Africa

Za'alya was in a cabin in the deep woods, trying her best to hold back from screaming. She loved the pleasure and pain of rough sex. She laid on her back as her side piece entered her vagina with his thirteen inch monster dick, trying to loosen her up.

"Ahhh," he moaned, loving the wetness of her tight pussy. He started fucking her so good that her legs began to shake in the air.

Za'alya was squeezing the African man's chiseled, well-defined waist as she felt an orgasm explode. His huge dick stroked in and out of her warm wetness, spreading her vagina walls. Once he pulled out, creamy juices were pouring out of her neatly-trimmed pussy. It was small with a clit that looked like a pink pearl.

With another round in her, she placed his dick in her warm mouth. Her thick wet lips sucked it slowly while she was bent over rubbing her clit, wishing someone else was behind her. She loved to get gangbanged. It made her cum so hard.

After getting his large dick standing tall again, she positioned herself above him and lowered herself on his dick with ease.

"Ummm," she moaned as she began to slowly ride the massive dick. She immediately began to yelp as his dick disappeared inside of her. She moved in a steady rhythm. She was screeching and jerking her body into an orgasm while she bounced her phat ass up and down on his dick, making her ass clap on his thighs.

The African man had to buckle down to the bed as she increased the pace. The man moaned something in his

Ndebele language as he came inside of her. Her titties bounced up and down in his face.

Seconds later, Za'alya climaxed again, leaving his semi-hard dick covered with thick cum.

She stood up and began to get dressed in a black strapless dress and heels. She looked beautiful, as if she was going on a date.

The man put on his blue garment, covering his whole body. He was a handsome young African man with a six pack, big dick, and nice smile – just her type.

"When can I see you again?" the man asked as he put on his sandals.

"I can't really say. This may be the first and the last," she replied, knowing that his tribe and her tribe were enemies. That was why she always sneaked to other villages to have orgies and sex: because she loved the thought of fucking the enemy. It gave her a rush.

Za'alya was a big freak. She loved to get fucked. But in her tribe, it was a death sentence to fuck before marriage, so she would go in other villages and let them run trains on her. There was one time in Kadoma where she let eight dudes have their way with her and she loved it. Za'alya had just met this young man three hours ago, seduced him, and it was on after that.

"I live here, so you are welcome to come back," he said.

She looked around the small cabin to see a bathroom in the corner, a stack of logs to make fire with to cook, wood chairs that were handmade, swords, bamboo sticks holding the cabin in place, and his mattress on top of stacked hay.

"Yeah, but no thank you. But you have nice swords," Za'alya said as she grabbed one off the wall admiring it. Before he could even reply, Za'alya quickly swung the sword, slicing open his neck. Blood squirted all over the dirt floor.

Za'alya laughed and walked out of the small cabin, unaware that the young man she was just having unprotected raw sex with had full-blown AIDS. She was unaware that he had just gotten the last laugh and she just did him a favor.

***

Staten Island, NY

Big Smokey had just arrived at his auto body shop early Sunday morning. Normally it was closed, but he wanted to drop some money off in his office safe as he normally did every four days.

Life for Big Smokey was great. He had two mansions: one in North Hamptons, where P. Diddy lived, and another home in Westchester County near Peekskill and Ossining. He had a couple of businesses, real estate for sale, car lots, and had Staten Island on lock thanks to his Capo Dex, who ran the city with an iron fist.

Big Smokey was on the phone with one of his baby mothers as he walked into his shop. He turned on the lights to see broken cars parked everywhere and on lifts. His shop was a busy shop Monday-Saturday. Not only did he have the best mechanics in the city, but the lowest prices.

"Rain, listen, I just paid you child support and gave you an extra two bands for yourself. That's not even my position, bitch, you not sucking my dick," Big Smokey talked into his iPhone as she began yelling. "Bitch, disrespect? You shitting me, ma. You been disrespected yourself when you fucked my ops, called police on me, put me on child support, and took my son from me, so you better call that nigga who dick you is sucking and ask him for change if he got it, you washed up, cum sucking bitch!" He went in on her, then hung up.

Big Smokey walked into his office, turning on the light switch on the side of the wall, only to be surprised.

"Yo, what the fuck!" Big Smokey yelled.

"Surprise, nigga!" his brother Sheek said with a gun pointed at him and fire in his eyes.

Sheek was his blood brother, a year older than him. He just did ten years in the feds in Big Sandy camp and Canaan camp prison. He used to be a big dawg in the streets, a known killer, until he got caught for a body and ratted. He snitched on his crew, his uncles, and best friends, giving a lot of them life sentences after he took the stand eight times.

He never told on Big Smokey, his little brother, so he never understood why his brother cut him off and never sent him money, pics, or letters, never visited his kids. He felt disrespected. He knew what he did was wrong, but he had to save himself, and he rationalized that at least he didn't snitch on him.

"Sheek, what the fuck you want? This how we doing it now, hot-ass nigga?" Big Smokey stated, pissed off, looking at his brother. He had gained at least eighty pounds of muscle and had no neck. He was 6'6" and 309 pounds and Smokey was 6'5" 270 pounds - big, black and ugly - but both men looked alike.

"Nigga, this is payback. You think I'ma let you play me like a bitch nigga? I fucking made you, fam. Without me, you wouldn't have none of this!" Sheek shouted with tears rolling down his face. He stood up with the pistol pointing at his brother's face.

"Sheek, you told on Uncle Ron, a nigga who showed ya the game and raised you. Loyalty before royalty, my nigga," Big Smokey said.

"Nigga, what?" He laughed. "You think you always had shit figured out, huh? Well, let me tell you a little about Uncle Ron before I kill your sucker ass," Sheek said.

Big Smokey knew he was only seconds away from meeting Allah because his brother was a gangsta killa rat. Big Smokey had a 9mm in his back, but he knew his chances at getting to it were zero because Sheek was watching his every move with a P89 Ruger in his hand.

"Good ole Uncle Ron fucked my baby mother and got her pregnant. So you think I was going to let that rock, nigga? Hell no!" Sheek said, checking the time on his G shock watch he had in prison. He was just released two days ago and he knew his mom knew where his brother worked, so he asked her for his info so he could rebuild his bond with him. She gladly agreed and gave him this main shop location.

"So you sold ya honor all over some pussy that couldn't even send ya a dollar in the joint, my nigga? Come on, Sheek, you were always an official breed. Put the gun down so we can talk," Big Smokey stated, trying to talk his brother out of his gun.

"Nigga, I look dumb? Shut the fuck up! I been dreaming of the day I could come here and murder your ass," Sheek said, smirking.

A'ight, nigga, do you, fuck nigga. You a cold-blooded rat anyway. I'ma see you in hell. Once ya snitched, we were never brothers after that, but I'm just mad I let a rat kill me," Big Smokey said, really pissed. His life was flashing before his eyes.

"See you there."

Click...click...click.

The gun jammed as Sheek pulled the trigger. He forgot that the P89 Desert Eagles always jammed.

Big Smokey wasted no time. He flew into action and pulled out his 9mm.

Bloc! Bloc! Bloc! Bloc!

Big Smokey saw Sheek's body drop back, falling over the table as he took his last breath. Big Smokey put two bullets in his face, ending his brother's life without any remorse.

Big Smokey called Dex so he could get a clean-up crew to get rid of the body.

Chapter 11
Miami, FL

Brandon was in martial arts class, watching two of his friends go round for round in Muay Thai as their trainer shouted out words of encouragement to his students. One of them hit the other with a powerful blow to the head, which dazed him he crawled to get up.

"Halt!" shouted Mr. Ching as he walked over to the fighters. "The self is the friend of a man who masters himself through the self, but for a man without self-mastery, the self is like an enemy at war. Franky, you must master yourself. You are your own worst enemy. When you can figure out how to master and control your self-mastery, come back," Mr. Ching said, dismissing the student.

Brandon was shocked that one of the best fighters was put on time out. Franky was one of the best in his class.

"I can't believe this shit, Brandon! That wasn't even a real match, bro. We were only practicing!" Franky shouted after class was over and the two gathered their gear and their bags.

"You know how Mr. Ching is. Don't even trip. But Holmes almost knocked you out. Mr. Ching might be trying to save your life," Brandon said, laughing.

"Bro, I had a long fucking day. I've been here since 8 a.m. in the morning training. That was a lucky hit. Shit!" Franky said, pissed off. Franky was a tall, skinny, blue-eyed kid with a long reach that had a 17-1 winning streak.

"Okay, Franky, and I'm Shaq at the three point line. But hold on while I text my step-pops. I told him we were getting out at four, but he closing early today," Brandon said, looking at the clock on the wall, which read three o'clock.

"Oh aye, who was that mixed lady that came in here the other day, bro? Your sister is bad. She look like one of those girls on the cover of a magazine," Franky stated honestly.

"That's my mom, asshole."

"Oh man, I'm sorry, Brandon," he replied quickly. "There goes my ride. Do you want a ride home?" Franky asked.

"Hell no! My parents found out I got in a car with a white person, they'd kill me," Brandon stated, laughing but serious a little.

"I knew you were racist! But you got the same color eyes as us," Franky said. His mom was now parked in a minivan outside of the studio.

"Nah. I'm good. My ride is on its way," he replied as everybody was leaving with their families.

"Okay. I'll see you tomorrow," Franky said, climbing in the passenger seat. His mom looked like a school teacher.

Brandon received a text from Romell saying he would be there shortly. Mr. Ching talked to him for a couple of seconds, then went his way.

Brandon was the only one in the lot now. He sat on the bench watching a Jeep ride into the parking lot with tints. Brandon played on his phone, paying no attention to the vehicle slowly pulling up on him.

***

Big C had been in Miami for a couple of days. Shota sent him after he found a location on his nephew, thanks to his social media account. Shota was very wise and clever. He believed in an eye for an eye. It didn't take Shota long to strategize a full-blown plan because he knew and understood the logic of war.

Big C had been tailing Brandon and Romell for days and right now was the perfect time to put his plan into full effect. He had two other large Jamaican niggas with him, ready to work.

"He is alone. We just pull up on him and drag his little ass in the truck," Big C said, giving orders as if he was the boss.

Big C pulled up on the curb, parked, and hopped out with his two goons, approaching the kid.

"Hey…"

The kid looked up, wondering what was going on.

One of the men grabbed Brandon by his shirt, lifting him in the air as if he was a toy, but when Brandon realized what was going on, he kicked the man in his nuts. The man dropped Brandon and he did a spin kick into the other dread head's chest, making him stumble backwards. Big C had enough of this shit. There was a highway across the street and he knew people could see the commotion.

Big C pulled out a Taser and pricked Brandon in his neck from behind, shocking him to the ground. But out of nowhere, a small Chinese man ran on him and hit Big C with a four piece, making him fall to the ground.

The other two men went for the Chinese man. Mr. Ching started to beat the shit out of both men.

Mr. Ching had come back around to make sure his shop was closed and one of his students was still lurking around. When he saw Brandon getting attacked, he had to help him, even though he saw Brandon handling himself well.

When Brandon got up, he saw Big C pull out a big gun, but as soon as he reached to grab it, he used a tactic he learned years ago to disarm his opponents.

Two shots went off and Mr. Ching fell to the ground. One of the wild shots pierced his heart. Mr. Ching clutched his

chest, trying to breathe, but oxygen wasn't coming. He took his last breath.

Brandon was so caught up in the moment he didn't even see the butt of the gun slam into the back of his head, knocking him clean out.

The goons tossed him in the back seat and pulled off. All of them had busted lips, black eyes, and bloody noses.

Chapter 12
New York

Naya was standing up in an all-white cutout Prada dress with red bottoms on her manicured feet. The crew was all there, including the newest member Glizzy, who rocked an all-red Gucci suit and tie with his dreads hanging.

This was Naya's first Empire meeting since before she caught her federal bid for murder, drugs, and the biggest RICO indictment Jersey had ever seen.

The meeting was in Brooklyn at an old sewing shop they had owned for years thanks to Bam Bam before he was murdered.

"Wow, this shit feels crazy! Months ago, I would never think of being here around y'all with the people who was with me and Brazy since day one, feel me?" Naya said, sitting down at the head of the long table in the middle of the empty dusty warehouse. "I know I've been gone for a while, but it's cool because I'm more than updated on all of our current events. First off, y'all niggas are all rich as shit now. I remember when Glizzy was in Atlanta selling eight balls and Red Hat was trying to snatch purses and shit," she said, making everybody laugh.

"She just put a vicious bond on a nigga," Red Hat said, smiling.

"Shit, nigga, I heard you was a phone snatcher back in the day," Bullet said, laughing.

"Now we all are millionaires. It's crazy how life works. We made it through hard times and y'all even had more hard times when I was gone. Given the same amount of intelligence, timidity will do a thousand times more damage in war then audacity, so I respect everyone at this table. We all have something valuable that we bring to the Empire.

That's why we all here. I believe Allah connected us for a reason," Naya stated, looking around the room.

"That's a fact, sis. But on the real, son, I've got every hood still looking for PYT. I don't think she just disappeared. Something is up and somebody knows something. We all know she did a lot of dirt, like she did a lot of serious shit, but we all knew she would never go out without a fight. Everybody knows how they get down," Red Hat said, making a point.

Naya was silent. She didn't want to hit this subject, at least not yet, because it always touched a soft spot in her heart. "We going to look into it. I'm speaking to Rugar too, but it's been over two years."

"You know what? I remember she used to always say something bad was coming. I wonder if she knew this was going to happen," Big Smokey stated, making everybody think back, remembering her say the same shit.

"Give me some time, gentlemen. I'ma get to the bottom line, Blood," she said. Her emergency phone vibrated in her Prada purse on the table. She had left her personal phone outside in the car. Only four people had the emergency phone number, so she knew it was something serious. "Excuse me, y'all, emergency call," she said, pulling out her and phone walking off.

"Holla. What? No! How? Are you sure? Please, no! I'm on my way back now," Naya said as her eyes got glossy.

"What's up?" Twin asked, seeing Naya crying, which was unheard. He knew something serious just happened.

"Someone just kidnapped my son in Miami. I have to go," she said, rushing out and grabbing her purse as they followed her. But she told them to stay up top. She had to get to the airport as fast as possible. She had been scared of this day for years. This is why she always kept him hidden in Jersey.

With the life she and Brazy lived, they knew it was best to keep him underground because the game was cold and nobody played by rules. If Brandon was hurt, the whole city of Miami was about to experience a storm they had never seen before.

***

Zimbabwe, Africa

PYT was sitting on her thin mattress, waiting on her lunch, reading a book. The book was called *The Templars* and the assassins in it reminded her so much of herself that she felt like the character.

She heard the doors open. Two men walked inside without a tray in their hands, smiling. One of the men had a pole in his hand while the other one checked out the door, making sure nobody else was coming.

Both men were skinny Zimbabwean men with gowns only covering their lower bodies. The taller one looked nervous as he pulled out a sword and a key. He unlocked the cage and they both rushed her. PYT fought them off until the pole slammed into her head, dropping her as she passed out.

The men took turns raping PYT while she was unconscious. They had been thirsty for her even though they knew she was off limits. But she was so sexy the two couldn't resist.

One man was fucking her in her pussy. It was so tight he couldn't get all the way in, but he got in enough to nut in three minutes.

The other man was waiting his turn as he watched his cousin bust his nut on her thighs. His dick was extra hard as he watched him fuck the unconscious bitch he dreamed about.

When his cousin stood up, it was his turn. He rammed his dick in and out of her wet pussy, which was full of sticky pre-cum.

"Ummm," he said, nutting inside of her.

But he was unaware that four tribal men had walked in with her tray of food, catching the man inside of her letting out the last drop of cum. Her pussy was amazing. He was stuck.

The four men rushed in the cage with their swords and attacked both men, stabbing them viciously until blood flooded the cell. When both of the men were dead, they dragged their bodies out and locked her cage.

PYT woke up five minutes later to see puddles of blood everywhere in trails. She only remembered getting knocked out, but when she realized she was half naked, she looked at her pussy and legs to see thick cum everywhere.

Once her pussy started to hurt, she began to cry. She had been raped. Never in a million years did she think she would be raped and defenseless.

She wasn't even in the mood to eat. She just went to the sink to wash the cum out of her pussy while crying, wishing she was dead.

Chapter 13
Newark, NJ

Twin parked his Honda in front of the public park, pissed off. Coke, his capo, called him at 1 a.m. saying he needed him to come down to the late night spot, which in code meant hide out behind the public park where they grew up, but he knew the reason.

Twin was in some young pussy, a twenty-year-old bitch home from college looking for a good time, and Twin gave it to her young ass. She already couldn't get enough of the ballin'. He took her Honda down to the park instead of one of his luxury cars.

Once in the back, there was a small lake. Four of his Blood homies surrounded one nigga with pistols in a pitch black area

"Coke, what's popping? Thank you for the help, all of you," Twin said, looking at the men who he went to school with and whom he used to beat up after school every day. "Well, well, well Officer Froster - or Mikey, whatever they call you nowadays," Twin said, looking into the swollen eye of the officer.

He had been kidnapped hours ago coming out of a bar. Coke and his crew beat the shit out of him the whole ride to the park just because they hated cops.

"Marcus, come on, please, you know I'm a cop. Just let me go before this shit gets big," the man said, spitting out blood on the smelly grass while everybody laughed.

"Threats from a man who used to run home every day after school." He laughed. "Look, I'ma get to the point. I know you and your captain been trying to bring my crew down, but y'all can't. You and him have become a headache. Following me, watching my projects, photos, wiretaps, and undercover

informants. So now it's time I show y'all who you all really fucking with," Twin said, pointing his gun in his face.

"Please don't kill me," the cop moaned.

"I won't. But look, I want you to kill Captain Raymond," Twin said, pulling the gun away from his face, tucking it in his back.

"What, man? Are you crazy? I can't do that!" Officer Froster stated, looking at Twin as if he had lost his mind.

"Oh yes you can, and you will, my nigga. This is why," Twin said, pulling out a burnout cell phone and dialing a number. When the phone answered, he passed it to him.

"Daddy, Daddy, Daddy help us!" was all Officer Froster heard before Twin snatched the phone back. Twin had his wife and daughter held hostage across town in a low-key location.

"So what do you say now, tough guy" Twin asked, smiling hard.

"Please, Marcus, I can't kill the captain. If I get caught, I'll do life in prison," he said, crying, thinking about his five-year-old daughter's voice.

"You're a cop. You'll get away with it," Twin said.

"I can't," he replied while Coke slapped him with the pistol.

"Okay. I thought it would come to this," Twin said, dialing another number and passing him the phone again.

At first he was too scared to take it and his hand started to tremble.

"Baby, what's going on? Mommy and Granny love you. What have you got us into? These men aren't going to hurt you, are they? Baby, please do as they say," his mom said.

Officer Froster started crying like a baby. Twin hung up, now looking at him with a serious face.

"The ball is in your court, Blood. You take him out, or we take your family out. And don't try to run or go to your co-

workers. I will have a wire on you at all times. One funny move, you're dead, nigga and your whole family too. So what's your plan?" Twin asked.

"Okay, I'll do it. Just give me some time," Officer Froster stated, wiping his tears, knowing his life was now over.

"Nice doing business, family. See you later," Twin said, walking off to go back to fucking his new young freak.

***

Staten Island, NY

Big Smokey had just come from his brother's funeral with his mom, who was heartbroken from having to bury her oldest son - and her favorite son, at that.

Mrs. Cornwell was a heavyset black woman who used to be a school teacher. She was raised in Alabama, so she was an old school country girl.

"Smokey, I loved that boy. I know he wasn't perfect by far, but he was still my baby and your brother," Mrs. Cornwell stated as the limo drove though the mean streets of S.I. on a nice sunny breezy day.

"Yeah, Mama, this is just the life we chose. You raised us well. I can never take that from ya."

"I knew that, chile, but you want to know something? I find it odd that the day before he was found dead, he wanted to speak to you and I gave him your work address. He seemed very impatient about talking to you for some reason, son. I just wished you two could have talked before he was killed," she said, looking her son in his eyes.

"I wish we could have talked too," he replied, looking out the window, trying to avoid eye contact with his mother.

"Smokey, I'ma give you a special jewel I learnt years ago, son, and please take it with you in life. A person's eyes can tell a story before they say something," she said, smiling at him and turning her head.

"I know, Mama. Do you want to come to my house with the grandkids, or you want to go home?"

"Home, please. I'll be back tomorrow for Sunday dinner. Tell the kids I love them," she said as the limo entered the gated community where they both lived.

Big Smokey bought a house for his mom and himself on the same block years ago. He loved his mom and hated to see her sad, but he knew she understood the game, and snitches get stitches was the law of the land in the ghetto of America. He lived by it - blood or not.

Chapter 14
Santiago de Cuba, Cuba

Rugar was taking a walk in his big backyard, enjoying the tropical wind of the dry season. Whenever he would have a lot on his mind, he would go for a walk through the vineyard toward the woods in his backyard that looked like a forest.

Yesterday, Naya called him crying, telling him Brandon was kidnapped the other day after he left his marital arts practice class. He told her he would be on his way down there tomorrow first thing in the morning. Rugar thought it was just some hood niggas who just wanted some ransom money, knowing Romell had it. Romell had Brandon with him daily so that could have made him an easy target, of course. He thought it would get handled soon after a couple of bodies popped up.

Just as he made it to the end of the yard, he heard the bushes in the woods make noise as if someone was creeping in his woods.

"Who the fuck is there?" Rugar yelled as he pulled out a 50 cal pistol.

"Papi, wait, don't shoot, please!" An older man stepped from behind the bushes with his hands up, wearing a camouflage outfit.

Rugar thought the man looked familiar, but he couldn't put his finger on it. The man had long silky gray hair in a ponytail and was clean cut.

"Who the fuck are you?" Rugar said, ready to shoot, but something in the man's face was stopping him

"I'm Black Mist, the man who saved your life years ago when the Africans tried to kill you," the man said slowly.

"Oh shit, yeah, man, thank you. I never got the chance to thank you," Rugar said, lowering his gun.

"No problemo, my friend," Black Mist stated.

Black Mist was a legend in Cuba and other parts of the world. He was one of the best assassins in South and North America. He was also Hagar's brother.

"Why are you in the bushes? You could have come through the front. Is everything okay?" Rugar asked, now wondering why an assassin was in his bushes like a tree jumper or a sniper.

"I don't use doors. I'm very swift. I'm here for a reason – actually, a couple, my friend. Please take a walk with me," he asked Rugar. They stood on a trial for walking through the quiet woods.

"What's up?" Rugar said, walking with him, already fucking up his Stacey Adam shoes.

"I know PYT killed my sister because of your affair. Hagar was a dangerous, evil woman. You don't have to be alarmed. Only few know, and I forgive your wife since years ago, Hagar killed my wife and only son. She thought I never knew. It hurts till this day. I loved my wife and only child," Black Mist stated in a low-pitched voice, somewhat getting emotional.

"Damn," was all Rugar could say.

"I could have killed her many times, but I just didn't have it in me. But when PYT killed her, it was a big relief in my soul," he said, taking a deep breath in. The air smelled like cut grass and trees.

"I'm sorry about the whole event on my behalf and my wife's," Rugar stated sincerely.

"Okay, but that's not my main reason here," he said, stopping and giving him a serious look. "I believe I know where PYT is being held at and if I'm correct, then we're up against a serious, deadly man. But me and him have a little

history," Black Mist said, thinking about a man whom he truly hated.

Rugar paused. He had thought PYT was alive, but now he knew his instinct wasn't playing with him for two years.

"Where is she?" Rugar asked, ready to kill a whole country to get his wife back.

"In Africa with her father and sister. She is believed to be next up on the throne. I will try to find her. Most likely she is still alive. I know how their tribe operates. I used to work for them until things got out of hand with his brother - the one I killed," Black Mist stated.

"I got twenty million dollars for her to be brought back safely," Rugar said as Black Mist laughed

"Everything I do, I do it in respect for Jumbo, not for money. After this, I'm done. I'm really retiring this time. I'm dying of cancer. I have to go. I'll be in touch," Black Mist said, leaving Rugar standing there.

***

Miami, FL

Romell and Pressure were in one of Romell's clubs upstairs in the office, talking about daily events and business arrangements with the pills of coke.

"They should be here any minute. The club opens in an hour. The kid is not the party type, but I'm telling you, this nigga is 55% of our street profit," Pressure stated.

"You talk about him all the time. He must be a gold mine," Romell said, sitting down, drinking a cup of Black Henny. He was really thinking about Naya. Since her son's kidnapping, she had been in a silent phase on some crazy shit. He had never seen her like this.

"Here they go now," Pressure said.

Jalee came in with a beautiful woman wearing a dress and heels on his arm.

"What's good?" Pressure said, embracing Jalee and smiling while looking at his dime piece. Her eyes were different and she was foreign. Pressure nodded his head as he closed the door behind them both, getting a quick look at her phat ass.

"This is Jalee and his girl," said Pressure.

"Wife; but nice to meet you. I heard lots of things about you," Jalee said. He was rocking a two-piece Tom Ford suit because he and Hosayni had plans to go out to dinner after Pressure introduced him to the boss.

"Likewise. You doing your thing, and if I may say, your wife is beautiful," Romell said respectfully.

"Thank you," Jalee said as they all took a seat

Romell couldn't help but see something in Hosayni's eyes that was too familiar. It hit him that she had the same color eyes as his wife, which was rare.

"This is the future of the family, Romell. Trust me," Pressure said, texting China.

"I see. So where you from, shorty?" Romell asked,

"D.C.," Jalee said.

"Northeast?" Romell asked.

"No question," Jalee said, proud of his trey seven homies, who were crazy around his way.

"That's what's up. How long you been in Miami?" Romell asked, just trying to get to know him because he liked the kid's presence. It was strong.

"Just a new start. My family was into a lot of bullshit and I'm about money, so I got married to Hosayni and came to Miami and started from the bottom," Jalee stated.

"Question. Not to get off subject, but are you both Muslims? Your names are Islamic," Romell asked.

"Yeah, we both born Muslims," Jalee stated, wondering what that had to do with the meeting.

"Okay. As-salaam-alaikum. My whole family Muslim," Romell stated.

"Wei alaikum salaam," Jalee and Hosayni said.

Hosayni sat there quietly with her legs crossed. Both of the men seemed okay, but there was something about Romell that rubbed her the wrong way.

"Pressure, her and Naya got the same eyes. You're the second person I ever seen with those types of eyes," Romell said to Hosayni.

She said nothing, letting the name Naya replay in her thoughts. It sounded familiar, but she knew there were a thousand Nayas in the country.

"I don't want to hold you up. Me and my wife got a date," Jalee said, sitting up.

"I got a flight to New York with Naya. This Empire shit got her busy at the wrong time, Pressure, but them niggas on one, bruh, especially Red Hat," Romell said, talking to Pressure, who was texting.

"Excuse me?" Hosayni said, thinking she just heard wrong. She had a crazy look in her face that everyone saw.

"Oh, nothing, I was talking to Pressure, but thank you for coming out. It was nice meeting the both of you," Romell said, smiling.

Pressure led Jalee and Hosayni out. The two men talked about how they liked Jalee, but his wife was weird. They would be sure to tell him to leave her at home next time.

Hosayni's blood was boiling. She knew Romell and Pressure had connections to the Empire, and she explained everything to Jalee. She couldn't believe it.

Chapter 15

Atlanta, GA

Glizzy was in a club in the VIP section alone today, just trying to live his best life.

Since being a part of the Empire, he had been moving on a new level with a thicker crew, flooding the inner city with bricks and opening businesses. Naya told him that now since he was a part of the Empire, he would have to clean up some of his dirty money. Glizzy went and opened two car washes, a studio, a plumbing company, and clothing store.

The club was a little dark tonight and was jam packed because a couple of Atlanta rappers had performed and Waka Flocka was in the building.

Glizzy was bopping his head to the beat of a Cardi B song, "Bodak Yellow", when he saw a bad white bitch walk in the club looking like Kylie Jenner in a white Balmain dress with diamonds around her neck and wrist. Even Glizzy's security outside of the red ropes saw her come in.

"Yo, Champ, go get her and invite her over here with me," Glizzy told one of the five guards he rolled with 24/7.

"Okay, boss," Champ said, going after the chick. She was now standing at the bar as every nigga in the club eyed her.

Glizzy saw Champ pointing towards him and talking, then he saw the women shrug her shoulders and follow him.

Glizzy stood up and lifted the rope for her when he saw her long blonde hair, bright blue eyes, perky breasts, nice round ass, and petite frame. His dick got hard because she had sex appeal.

"Hey, thank you for coming. I'm Glizzy. I saw you and had to have you - at least for a while," he said, smiling, making her blush.

"Oh yeah? Well thank you, I guess. What you doing by yourself?" she asked with an accent that was different to Glizzy. He figured she was from the East coast.

"Waiting for you. Do you drink?"

"No thank you, not tonight. I came to have fun, you know?" she said, licking her lips liking what she saw.

"What type of fun?"

"The type of fun that will have you stalking me," she said, smiling.

"So why are we still here?" he said, eyeing her.

"I was going to ask you the same shit."

"Let's go," he said.

They both stood up. When he saw her nice little phat ass again, he couldn't wait.

Thirty minutes later, the two were in the hotel naked.

Glizzy grabbed her hips tightly and started to suck her big clit poking out of her small, pretty, shaved pink pussy. His tongue was against her clit, driving her crazy. The longer she felt the stimulation, the louder her moans became.

"Ohhh!" She tried to push his hand and head away to break free because she was cumming back to back. After she came, she sat up, unable to get up because her legs were wobbly from the oral sensation.

Glizzy smiled and made her stand up. As he ate her, out two fingers went in and out of her pussy. He was going up and down, left and right, and back to sucking on it. She couldn't step the drip from flowing.

"Ummm…" She breathed erratically, which was like her heartbeat, while she came all over his hands.

"You taste good," he said, sucking her small pink nipples.

She took the head of his big ten inch dick and rubbed it against her clit while her muscles contracted. He grabbed her hips and eased himself into her tight pussy. She started to

grind and rotate against his hips while the TV silenced her loud moans. He started thrusting faster and faster as she got wetter and more excited, taking all ten inches as he was hitting every spot.

"Ugh...fuck me!" she screamed as she spread her legs wider and he continued to pound her pussy out.

After they both climaxed again, they needed a break.

"Damn, a nigga just might have to stalk you," he said, laughing. He was hot, tired, and sweaty."

"Yeah, that was good, but I only wish it would last forever," she said, putting on her bra and thong.

"It could, but I never caught your name," he stated, feeling dumb. "Okay, you're done already? We can chill here until the morning," Glizzy said, laying down shirtless in the bed.

"Nah, I'm okay."

"Do you want my number at least?" he said, feeling as if his dick game didn't please her.

"That won't be necessary," she said, pulling out a star knife and flinging it into his neck, killing him instantly. His blood squirted all over the wall and bedsheets.

Katie from the UK Cartel smiled and called her goons, who were parked outside. They had already killed Glizzy's guards who were all posted in a truck watching the room, waiting on him. Katie's guards were all swift assassins from London and well-trained. They used silencers to kill, or blades.

She was only in Atlanta to have fun, party, and get some dick. She never intended to sleep with Glizzy, but he approached her. She would normally fuck a nigga, then kill him. There was only one man she didn't kill, and that was Romell.

Katie never even caught Glizzy's name. She had no clue he was a part of the Empire. If so, she would have found another victim.

She left the hotel room smiling, glad to get her rocks off as she hopped in one of the two Benz trucks waiting on her.

***

Opa-Locka, Miami

Romell and Pressure were in the trenches in some buildings where Pressure's soldiers trapped out of, but this was Southside's neck of the woods.

Romell never came down to traps. He was like Ghost from the *Power* TV show: behind the drama. Romell was there because Pressure said it was an emergency, but when Romell saw the two Jamaicans tied up in the empty apartment that smelled like piss, he was confused. He had better shit to do then watch a nigga kill some Jamaicans.

"Why am I here, Pressure?" asked Romell, looking at the two men stare at him for mercy as six young boys with assault rifles surrounded them.

"Southside knows about your stepson getting kidnapped. Just so happens he was in Lil Haiti and these two dumb niggas was bragging about kidnapping a little kid who knew martial arts and that they killed his trainer. So Southside put two and two together," Pressure said as the room was silent.

"Where's my son?" Romell said coldly, staring at the two naked dread heads on the floor

"We got a call from our boss to do it, but we don't know where he is now," one of the men said. They had been hearing Romell's and Pressure's name for years and knew these men would kill a nigga's whole bloodline.

"Wrong answer. I'ma ask you one more time. Where is my son?" he asked.

"He with Shota of the Jamaican Cartel. We work for him. He sent his son down here to help us kidnap him, then they flew back to Jamaican with him. I swear, that's all we know. We go paid $100,000 to do it," the other man said, scared to death wishing, he never would have done it.

"Okay, thank you. I hope the 100,000 was worth your life," Romell said, walking out with Shota on his mind.

Pressure and his goons killed both men and got rid of their bodies, which was a day job for them.

Romell Tukes

Chapter 16
Atlantic City, NJ

Officer Froster sat behind the wheel of the all-black new Chevy Malibu, staking out Captain Raymond's two story house in a nice, suburban area on the outskirts of the city.

Froster was nervous as he picked up the small mirror in his passenger seat. He put a gram of coke in a line with a rolled-up dollar bill. He hit the line of coke, feeling the rush go straight to his brain. He leaned his head back while his nose started to run.

Froster couldn't believe Twin had him in a situation so tight that he was about to risk his life. He would do anything for his daughter and family, even if it meant killing his boss.

A couple of his co-workers warned him about snooping into Twin's business and trying to build a case because he would come up with nothing except a headache, and they were right.

It was eight at night, and all the lights were on in the house. Froster saw Captain Raymond's work car parked in the driveway, but only one person in the house, which was him, so he figured his wife was out somewhere.

Froster had come up with a plan to make a clean hit and get away. He hopped out and walked across the street, dressed in all black with a hat on.

***

Captain Raymond was an African-American man in his early 50's who was trying to clean up the streets of Jersey by locking up every gangbanger and drug dealer. Twin and his vicious crew were first on his list. He was so close to busting them. He could feel it in his soul. When Twin got indicted by

the Feds years ago, it was the best time of his life, but when he won his appeal and came home, he vowed to throw him under the jail this time.

Captain Raymond was about to call his son in Arizona when he heard the doorbell ring. He got up from his living room couch, wondering who it could be so late. He rarely had company.

Once at the door, he saw Froster standing on the other side of the peephole. He liked Froster. He was smart, a good kid, and he reminded him of himself at that age. He had invited Froster over to dinner twice. That was something he never did. But that's how he knew Froster knew where he lived.

"Froster, what's going on? You okay?" Captain Raymond asked, seeing a spooked look on Froster's face.

"I just need someone to talk to, boss. My daughter is sick and the doctor said she may not make it," Froster said, lying through his teeth.

"Damn it, come in, Froster. I'm sorry to hear that." Captain Raymond saw white residue of something powdery on his nose, but he kept it to himself as Froster walked inside.

"I don't know what to do. I can't live without my daughter," Froster said in a sad voice.

"We're going to get through this, trust me. I'll get you a drink," Captain Raymond said, walking to the kitchen to pour drinks.

"I hope so."

"I know you are. God is good." Captain Raymond walked back into the living room with two glasses full of Paul Mason. The sound of glass shattering could be heard as he walked into his living room.

"I'm sorry, boss, but I have to," Froster said with tears in his eyes. He looked up to Raymond, but he had to do this.

"Put the gun down, please. What has gotten into you? Let's talk about it," Raymond said, scared to death.

"I can't talk. They got my family. If I don't do this, they die," Froster said as his hands were shaking.

"Who? What are you talking about?"

"Twin, the kid we;ve been investigating. He got my family and their lives are in your hands."

"No, Froster, they're lying, we can get him. Now put the gun down."

"Sorry, Captain." Froster placed his finger on the trigger Boom! Boom!

Blood squirted all over the place, but it wasn't Raymond's blood.

Unbeknownst to Froster, the Captain's wife Sara was upstairs asleep the whole time until she heard glass break. When that happened, she went to the stairs to hear her husband having a conversation. She was eavesdropping from the top of the stairs. She heard everything word for word, but was unsure who it was. Without hesitation, she went and grabbed her husband's work gun and shot Froster twice in the back of the head.

Captain Raymond called it in. He looked at his wife in shock. She was crying, traumatized that she had just killed the man she was having an affair with.

***

New Delphi, India

The Shah Cartel family was run by Anna Pawson Shah. She was a beautiful woman in her mid-forties who looked twenty. She had a perfect toned body, but one would never see it unless they were family because she always wore

concealing garments. The one thing that stood out about her was her grayish green bright eyes.

She was a very powerful woman with a serious army full of terrorists originating from Pakistan. She supplied India, Burma, Nepal, Sri Lanka, and the Nicobar Islands with drugs. Since her country had the fourth largest reserves in the world for coal, she had a big profit in every coal company in her region. Her home sat in the middle of a mountain surrounded by mountains, wild animals, and volcanoes. Her castle was made up from cement, 7,891 square feet with 76 acres of her own land. India had a lot of droughts, floods, monsoonal rains, and earthquakes, but it was home for her. She had family in the States, but she kept that side of her family away from her dangerous lifestyle.

"Shah, sorry to disturb you, but we have found your daughter," a big Indian man said. He was wearing a suit. He entered Shah's colorful quiet room, which was filled with a lot of Hindu religion items everywhere.

The two talked in their Hindi language for a second before she stood up and went to her closet and grabbed some military assault rifles.

She was on her way to Africa to see a man she hated. She had given birth to a daughter with King Omen.

Anna Shah was mother to PYT and Naya. She was unable to raise them due to her position in the cartel, but she refused to let harm come to her kids. When she heard her daughter got kidnapped, she went crazy. She had a clue King Omen was the reason after she moved to New Jersey with Shah's stepsister. Now that she knew where her daughter was, she was going to get her. She prayed she was still alive, knowing what type of people Omen and Za'alya were.

Chapter 17
Miami, FL

Pressure was driving his Porsche down to the riverfront to speak to Jalee about some business plus. It was time for him to re-up.

Things were going well for him. His love life was at its best. He recently proposed to China and she accepted his marriage proposal before he even finished the sentence.

The drug game was starting to get old. He spoke to Romell about retiring in the next couple of weeks and he was all for it. That was another reason why he was on his way to see Jalee, so he could pass him his crown in the game.

Pressure had a strong liking for Jalee. It wasn't all about the money. It was very genuine since day one. He was going to give the game up, but he had to get everything in order first.

He pulled up next to Jalee's black Challenger, which was fresh. He nodded his head, liking his style. It was 10 p.m. and dark, but he was still able to see Jalee sitting on a bench next to the rail and water.

Normally people would be out taking walks on the board walks after going to the bars down the block around the corner but tonight it was empty and quiet.

***

Jalee was sitting near the water in deep thought. Since meeting Romell, his life had somewhat changed. He had to keep a distance until he figured shit out.

Hosayni explained to him everything she heard Muhammad talk about before he was killed. She knew it was members from the Empire. So he had to figure out how

Romell and them were connected because it could lead to his father's and the whole family's murderers.

He saw Pressure coming. He knew he had to play his cards right now to get the info he needed so he could finally sleep at night.

"What's up, bruh? Damn, nigga, where you been at?" Pressure asked, embracing him.

"I just been a little busy. You know how shit be, homie," Jamie said, sitting down.

"Yeah, of course, but I'ma have my crew drop off everything to you tomorrow morning, so be ready." Pressure looked at him not feeling the energy.

"A'ight, good, I'll be there."

"Facts. But I've been meaning to holla at you."

"Me too. I'm glad you came."

"Oh, okay, go first, li'l bro," Pressure said, knowing something was on his mind.

"How do y'all know them Empire niggas from New York? I was just wondering because I heard a lot about them cats," Jalee said calmly.

"Oh, we all family, they all solid, especially Ruger and Naya, bruh. Romell killed some Muslim nigga name Muhammad who was terrorizing Jersey and the East Coast. He did them a big favor for his wife, and ever since we been cool with them. Shit, my girl is Rugar's sister. It's a small world. Him and Naya run that shit," Pressure said proudly as Jalee was zoned out. "You good?" he said, noticing his awkward look.

"Yeah," he said coldly.

"Shit, I can link ya with them next time we all get up. They come down to Miami daily," he said when suddenly he felt cold steel to his head

"You motherfuckers killed my family," Jalee said, now standing with his gun to his head.

"Who, man? You fucking tripping. This how it is?"

"Yeah, nigga, Muhammad my pops."

"Nigga, fuck your pop! Do what you gotta do," Pressure said, spitting in his face.

Bloc! Bloc! Bloc! Bloc!

Jalee felt gunpowder burn his hand. Without time to waste, he dragged Pressure's body and tossed it in the river. A trail of blood could be seen.

He ran off, leaving his body floating in the river. As he pulled off, he saw cars coming towards the lot, people coming to take a walk or enjoy the stars and water. It was a beautiful night in Miami.

***

Zimbabwe

PYT was sitting on the cold cement floor waiting for dinner. She had just gotten done exercising for two hours and she was starving.

Her sister came down to see her early and she was teasing her with food as she talked shit to her for an hour before she went out of town.

Every night she thought about Rugar. She feared being raped again, starving to death, and dying without being with Rugar. She knew nobody had a clue where she was at. She was in a forest surrounded by a jungle. Who would ever find her? There were times when she wanted to kill herself, but she stayed strong.

PYT heard someone picking a lock, which alerted her because all the guards had keys. She jumped up and ran to the bars, ready to fight.

Within seconds, a woman ran in dressed in an all-black garment covering her face except her eyes. When PYT saw the woman, her heart froze. There was something very familiar about her eyes.

"Who are you?" PYT asked as she saw the lady trying to open her gate.

"Your mother. I'm getting you out of here," the woman, who was Anna Shah, said with her soft voice.

PYT felt tears coming down. She didn't even question her. The woman's eyes said it all. They were just like hers and her sister Naya's.

"Come on; cry later .We have to go, I don't want nobody to get wind of anything funny. All the guards are spread throughout the woods. I just killed six of them," she said, finally getting the gate open.

"Thank you," PYT said, hugging her mother who was also crying.

PYT was barefoot with a gown. She ran out the door leading into an underground tunnel, which was pitch black, as her mom led the way. Once at the end, there were stairs leading to outside in front of King Omen's home. They both climbed out of the underground tunnel. They placed the small wooden door with grass on it to camouflage it into the ground with the low cut grass.

It was so dark that they saw nothing. They were about to run through the woods and jungle until they heard a voice that sent a shock through their bodies.

"Going somewhere, Zeema? And it's a pleasure to see you, Shah," King Omen said, coming from behind a tree as

ten Africans with swords appeared from behind the trees, surrounding both women.

"I won't let you brainwash my daughter," Shah said with a sword in her hand as she stood in front of PYT, protecting her.

"You got two other daughters, Shah. This one is mine, and you can die here with her," he said, pulling out two blades.

She knew how deadly he was with blades. She had been forced to leave her crew of killers across the jungle because it could have alerted the guards. She was in the woods for four hours watching their movements. That's how she knew PYT was underground under the wooden floor.

"So be it, Omen. I die in honor," she said firmly.

"Still the same," he said with a laugh. He rushed her with his blades as she stood her ground, ready to work her blade.

All of a sudden an arrow shot right through King Omen's forehead, dropping him in slow motion as the guards looked around. Arrows started to rip through all of their bodies one by one as the rest ran off for dear life.

Shah and PYT stood there confused until they saw the man who saved their life appear from the woods, dressed in all black, with bow and arrows strapped to his chest and back.

"You saved us. Thank you," Shah said trying to figure out who he was, because killing King Omen was something nobody had the balls to do.

"I know you," PYT said, staring at him

"I'm Black Mist, but no need to thank me at all. Me and your father had a long rivalry. We can consider us even. PYT, I know you know who I am talking about," he said with a smirk.

She wasn't smiling. She wondered how he knew she killed Hagar.

"The famous Black Mist. I heard a lot about you. Thank you again," Shah said, ready to leave.

"Rugar awaits you, PYT. I'm sure your mother can lead you back. I'm retired now, so I'm sure you will never see me again. Take care," he said, disappearing again.

"We have to go, and I have to explain everything to you. This isn't a good way to reconnect with your daughter" Shah said, walking through the jungle and woods.

It was at least seven or eight miles of walking until they touched the main land. They heard hyenas, lions, and all types of wild animals hunting prey while making loud noises.

PYT was happy to meet her mom again. She didn't even remember the last time she had seen her, but she was even happier to be free after close to three years in captivity.

Chapter 18
Mayabeque, Cuba

Savannah laid in her king-sized bed wearing nothing as she placed two fingers in her pussy. She plunged her fingers in and out her as she leaned her head back.

"Ummm, papi, Rugar," she moaned as her fingers went faster, coating her fingers with thick cum as she slid in with ease, touching her tight walls. "Fuck me...hard. Choke me," she groaned as she rubbed her small clit while sucking on her other index finger as if it was a dick.

"I'm cumming. Ugh!" she screamed as she squirted in the air. It was splashing everywhere for thirty seconds as she played with her clit until she was done.

Savannah was out of breath as she got out of her bed, looking at her soaked sheets, which she had to change twice a day.

Every day she masturbated to Rugar's pictures, which she had all over her room even on the ceiling. She had it so bad he stalked her dreams.

She had been plotting ways to get him to fall into her web, but nothing was working for her. He barely even talked to her when she came around. But she knew there was a way.

***

New York City
FBI Headquarters

"Mrs. Sanders, are you sure everything you just told me is 100% accurate?" Agent Lopez asked.

"Yes. I know he is a part of this drug trafficking Empire. He runs a big gang as well. He is destroying his community and killing civilians," she said.

"Why wait this long to report this to us? The Empire has been a cold case for years now and we are concerned they disappeared," Agent Berkeley said, sitting in the interrogation room, listening to the lady tell it all.

"These people are even stronger now than before. I believe they even could be connected to some cartels. I'm not dumb. I know the streets. I was a hustler's wife for over two decades!" she yelled, frustrated

"Listen, Miss, we can't open a closed case unless you have something we can go off of. I'm sorry," Agent Lopez said, sensing this woman was going to be a big problem.

"I thought you might say that," she said, reaching into her big purse to pull out a stack of photos of a nigga walking into Big Smokey's body shop and looking around. Then there was a photo of Big Smokey coming out of the shop. She had pics of six men dragging out a body bag with a body in it and tossing it inside of a white van.

"That's him they're dragging. My son," she said with tears, pointing at the picture of the body bag.

Both agents looked at each other.

"So your other son is the one who killed him? How you know it wasn't the six men that went in there?" Agent Lopez asked.

"I know my son Big Smokey. He hates rats and his brother ratted. But that doesn't make it right to kill his brother," Big Smokey's mother said.

"Okay, that's enough, Mrs. Sanders. We are going to open the case back up, but you have to be willing to take the stand at the grand jury," Agent Berkeley stated

"I will, with my head high."

"We'll be in touch," Agent Lopez said, walking out with his co-worker. "What do you think?" Agent Lopez asked.

"We are about to open up a can of worms. I'll go report it to D.C.," Agent Berkeley said, walking off. He was above Lopez in the Bureau and he was a house nigga. Lopez hated him.

Agent Lopez was the brother of the leader of the Mexican Cartel and their connection to the Empire was strong. He knew he had to do something before it was too late and that old bitch blew his cover. The Empire name hadn't been mentioned for years because they were lying low - until now thanks to a bitch in her feelings about her rat-ass son.

***

The next day

Mrs. Sanders was at home in the mini mansion Big Smokey bought for her years ago. She played gospel music throughout the house while she cleaned, something she did every Sunday before she had dinner with her family.

The doorbell rang, taking her out of her zone as she was cleaning the walls. She took off her gloves and went to the door to see Agent Lopez standing there in regular street clothes.

"Hey Agent, how can I help you? Come in," she said, letting him in.

He smelled the strong scent of bleach in the house. "I've got good news."

"Y'all got his black ass?" she said, happy they finally got her grimy son. She couldn't wait to take the stand on him.

"Yeah," he said, pulling out a gun and blowing her brains onto her clean walls before walking out.

Agent Lopez spoke to his brother and let him know the Empire was about to be under a big federal investigation, but that he was going to do what he could to prevent it because they were all connected.

***

Havana, Cuba

Rugar was at his new mansion in the capital of Cuba. The city of Havana was so beautiful and colorful. It brought people from all over the world just to visit.

The other day Naya had called him and told him that a Jamaican named Shota had Brandon and he was a Cartel leader. She claimed she met him years ago when she went on a vacation to Jamaica, but she had no clue why he would kidnap her son. Rugar promised to get to the bottom line of it, and today he was going to do just that.

He sat in his conference room upstairs. He dialed Shota's personal number and placed it on speaker. He sat there confused as to why Shota would play with his life like this.

"Hello," a Jamaican voice answered.

"Shota, this is Rugar. I believe you have something of mine."

"Yes, man, I do."

"So how do you want to do this?" Rugar asked, pissed off at his cocky attitude.

"You believe in a thing called karma?"

"Yeah, I do, but get to the point."

"You remember a kid named Lil C? I'm sure you do. Well, that was my grandson, and his father and I wanted blood and we got it," Shota said.

110

"Well, ya got the wrong person. I killed Lil C. Why not come for me, gangsta? Why go after little kids? Sounds like a true pussy boy to me."

"Oh, me gonna make sure me den get you good."

"Suck your mother's pussy! And he better be alive and well or I'ma bury your family in Jefferson City, Missouri and you cousins in Madison, Wisconsin," Rugar said, naming areas where Shota had a lot of family because he did his research.

"Touch me family and you're dead. Are we crisp?" Shota yelled, upset before hanging up in his ear.

Rugar had always felt something different about Shota. He just had a sneaky snake look that real niggas stayed away from because they already know the outcome.

Rugar already had teams of killers outside of seven of Shota's family member's homes in New York, California, Texas, Miami, and Wisconsin. He was about to spill so much blood that in Jamaica, there would be blood flooding warnings on Rastafarian TV's daily.

Romell Tukes

Chapter 19
Miami, FL

Naya was bent over on all fours, looking back. Her body vibrated back and forth as Romell fucked her from behind, banging her petite waist into his as her ass wobbled with every slam.

"Uhhhh...shit. Ummmm..." she mooned. She tossed her ass back as they fucked in the Season One hotel. "I love you!" she screamed as he rammed his whole pipe in and out of her.

Today was their anniversary so they went to a comedy show, dinner, and a weekend at a fancy expensive hotel.

Once he nutted, he pulled out and squirted on her phat ass. Her pussy looked swollen. She laid him down and rode his dick like a crazy cowgirl as her titties and hair flew everywhere. She felt him in her arteries. Within minutes, she climaxed on his dick, leaving it coated with her cum. She hopped off, placed his semi-hard dick in her mouth, and began sucking and slurping it, bopping her head up and down.

"Ohhh yes, suck it," Romell moaned. He fucked her warm mouth as she buried his dick down her throat.

When he came, she swallowed every drop, leaving nothing behind.

This was the first time she had sex in weeks because her mind was focused on getting her son back. She was in her own world.

"That was amazing, baby," Romell said, checking the Richard Mille watch that he dropped $1.4 million on weeks ago to go with his collection.

"Yeah, my body hurts. What time is it?"

"3 a.m."

"Damn, three hours straight and I ain't make you tap out?" she said, laughing.

"I almost did. I gotta go to Pressure's funeral in the morning downtown. That shit still fucking me up," he said sadly.

When Romell heard Pressure's body was found in the river, he was sick. Everybody loved Pressure. He couldn't even think of someone who would want to kill him.

"You want me to come?" she asked, lying in his muscular arms.

"Sure, if you want to, but I know you gotta link up with Rugar," he said.

"Yeah, I do. We gotta plan how we going to get our son back," she said, making him feel like a father.

"We will. Get some rest," he said, clapping off the lights as they fell asleep with violence on both of their minds.

***

Somewhere in the sky

Rugar was dazed, staring out his G5 jet window, unable to think straight or talk. He was in his pajamas on his way to New York.

He had received a phone call from PYT twenty minutes ago. He thought it was a joke, but it wasn't at all. He had tears in his eyes upon hearing her voice. She told him she was in New York with Red Hat, safe.

Without hesitation, he called his pilot and was now on his way to get his wife. He always had a feeling she was alive, even after three years. He couldn't wait to see her.

He looked at the fourteen guards on the plane asleep, thinking about Shota. He had already had most of his loved ones killed in a series of attacks. Although he feared their

retaliation, he had a plan. After he brought PYT home and got to the bottom of what happened, he planned to visit Jamaica.

***

Bronx, NY

PYT was in Red Hat's condo. She had arrived at his doorstep the previous night.

Her ride from Africa was long. Her mother brought her back to the States on a private jet, where the two had a long conversation. Her mom explained everything to her and she was surprised. She saw her mother at every Cartel meeting. She always wondered who the quiet lady was with the beautiful eyes. Not in a million years did she ever think it was her mom.

Shah explained to PYT that she played the distance to protect her children from dangerous shit like what just happened. She also explained to her that she had another sister somewhere out there younger than her and Naya.

"I'm so happy you alive, sis," Red Hat said, walking into his room to see PYT sitting on the couch watching the news on TV.

"Yeah, that shit was scary."

"They didn't hurt you, did they?" Red Hat asked, sitting down on his couch, watching her drink hot cocoa as she sat Indian style in a French jumpsuit.

"No, I was good," she said flatly, not wanting to tell anybody what really happened.

"That's what's popping. You missed so much," he said.

The doorbell rang. He knew Yasmine and Lyric were out running errands, so it had to be Rugar.

Red Hat went to open the door. He let Rugar inside. As soon as PYT heard his voice, she ran to him and jumped into his arms.

"Oh my God, I missed you so much!" she cried.

Rugar couldn't even say anything. It felt so good to hold his wife. He thought about the long nights. He had dreamed about this night.

The two talked in Red Hat's living room for two hours. She told him everything except about her being raped.

"Before we go home, I have to pay a visit to China to see Hubei. As I told you, he kidnapped me and gave me to my father," she said.

"Okay, let's go. I know where he at. He just texted me yesterday and his location was Tianjin, China. I have a couple of people over there who owe a big favor," Rugar said, making a call as they left Red Hat's condo.

***

Tianjin, China

Hubei was on his way to a meeting with a close friend, who was a crooked businessman just like him. He rode in a truck with three guards.

"What the fuck is that?" Mr. Hubei asked as he saw blue flashing lights behind him telling them to pull over. Hubei knew powerful people in the government, so him getting pulled over was disrespectful to him.

As soon as the two Chinese police came up to the window, the driver spoke their Shanghainese language.

The cops didn't respond. They both pulled out their work weapons and shot all three of Hubei's guards, killing them. They dragged Hubei out of the truck and tossed him in the

trunk of the police car after they shot him with a needle full of blue liquid.

***

A couple hours later

Hubei woke up with his body numb. He barely remembered what happened, but he could feel that he got hit with a powerful tranquilizer.

"The Hubei Cartel!" a female voice shouted from the darkness somewhere.

Hubei had no clue he was in a cargo warehouse on a large dock used for fishermen.

"Who's there? You have no clue who I am!" he yelled, slowly gaining his vision back as he heard heels clicking on the cement.

"You thought I would be dead by now, huh? Well, surprise!" PYT said, standing in front of him with a sword.

Hubei saw who it was and started to cry like a little girl. He couldn't believe who was standing in front of him. He was sure she would have been dead dealing with King Omen.

"Don't cry now," Rugar said, walking out from the back.

"How does it feel to be hit with some shit that can knock a horse out?" PYT said, laughing, playing with the sword on his face.

"Please, he made me do it. I had no choice."

"No...we all have choices. You don't even know what I went through because of you," she said with glossy eyes.

Rugar saw the pain in what she said and made a mental note to find out what really was going on in Africa, because she looked traumatized.

"I'm sorry, but I had to."

"Rule #4 of the commission: never cross another family member or harm them," PYT said.

She stabbed him in his neck and heart over 75 times. Rugar watched her lash out until he stopped her.

Rugar knew the two cops who pulled them over. They were from America and lived in Tianjin. He had saved their parents from getting murdered in New York years ago, so the two brothers told him they owed him one if he ever came to Tianjin. They held their word today.

PYT and Rugar walked out. She couldn't wait to do that to Hubei. But he wasn't the only who she was coming after.

Chapter 20
Jamaica, Kingston

"I told you I would find you. You're not really my target, but you'll suffice," Rugar said to Big C. He had him tied up in an abandoned building in the hardest hood in Kingston.

"My father's going to kill you," Big C said, in pain from the beating the Jamaicans put on him for two days straight.

Rugar put a one million dollar bounty on Big C's and Shota's head and within hours, Big C was tied up in the impoverished section of Kingston, where people barely had food to eat and clothes to wear.

PYT was home in Cuba, while Naya was in Port Kaiser hunting down Shota.

"Where is my nephew?" Rugar said, pointing a pistol with a 30 clip attached to it.

"I hope he dead, blood clot pussy boy!" Big C yelled as he hocked spit in Rugar's face.

He calmly wiped it. "That's your final answer, chump?" Rugar asked.

The dread heads were ready to collect their money. They all know who Shota was, but when it comes to money, they would kill their mothers.

"Fuck you! Suck your mother!" he spit before Rugar blew his brains all over the floor, then laughed.

He paid the dread heads one million in cash in a duffle bag. He then pulled over in two Range Rovers filled with his Cuban goons on his way to Naya so they could hunt for Shota, because they weren't leaving Jamaica until they found Brandon.

***

Port Kaiser, Jamaica

Shota was in his backyard smoking a big blunt of weed. He grew pounds of weed in his backyard.

This was his second house when he wasn't at his mansion. It was a big house with a farm and barn connected to the house. Mainly this house was used for growing weed and his barn was built into a prison for his victims, where he would inflict torture on his prisoner.

Brandon was in there surrounded by four Jamaicans at all times. He was told when to eat, shit, shower, or even move.

He had been trying to reach his son for two days now, but all he got was a voicemail. He figured he was stuck in some pussy somewhere.

Bob Marley could be heard throughout the house and backyard. He used his weed for meditation. Shota thought he heard a loud boom, but he paid it no mind as he continued to bop his head to the Bob Marley relaxing flow. As soon as the song got done, Shota felt cold steel pressed against his temple.

"Nice song," a kid's voice said.

Shota already knew who it was.

Brandon stood behind him with blood pouring out of his mouth and a ripped T-shirt.

When the guards were asleep outside of his cage where they had him like a dog, he was able to make a long line out of his bed sheets to fish out one of the sleeping guards' keys. Once he woke them, it was on and popping. He whipped all their asses and then killed them all and made his way to look for Shota.

"Put the gun down, kid. Let's talk," Shota said as his blunt fell out of his black, crusty lips.

"Turn around. You talk too much," Brandon said.

"I'll let you go, just——"

BOOM! BOOM!

Brandon shot him between his eyes and Shota's blood squirted on his face.

Brandon knew there were no other guards around, but he needed a phone and car keys. He didn't know how to drive, but he damn sure planned to get the fuck out of there.

He snatched Shota's phone and truck keys and dashed through the house. He made it to the front to see two blue Ranges. Brandon then saw four Range Rovers speeding up the steep uphill driveway.

Without hesitation, Brandon started busting at the trucks, killing one of the passengers in the first Range. He emptied the clip, killing the driver of the second truck as the Range crashed into a tree.

Brandon saw his mom hop out, running to him with tears, He ran to her, glad he didn't just kill her, but he had thought it was Shota's men.

"Oh my God! What happened? Where is Shota?" she yelled after hugging him.

Rugar ran up to him as he told his goons to go inside.

"Everybody dead," Brandon said.

Everybody paused, even the guards.

"What? You killed them all?" Naya asked, read to whip his little ass as she snatched away his gun.

"Yeah, Mom," he said nonchalantly.

"I'm glad you're okay. We love you," Rugar said, walking in the house to search the place while Naya and Brandon hugged and talked about what happened.

Minutes later, Rugar came back out with an awkward facial expression.

"He gave all of them head shots and he killed two of my men. It's time for you to go home," Rugar said, wondering if

Brandon ever had a clue he just killed seven people, and one of them was a very powerful man.

"Y'all not mad at me, are you?" he asked as he got in the truck.

"No. You have to defend yourself," Rugar said.

"Never kill again unless you have to, and don't tell nobody about what just happened – nobody. Erase it from your mind," his mom said looking at his busted lip.

"Okay."

"Your aunt can't wait to see you," Rugar said.

"PYT? I thought she was dead or whatever you said," Brandon said happy PYT was waiting on him.

"It don't matter. She back now," Naya said, smiling.

They took a private flight back to Miami and PYT flew out also. They all chilled at Romell's mansion, having a cook-out, happy everybody was there alive and well.

***

New York

Za'alya got off the plane. She had blond hair, sunglasses, tight Gucci jeans, and a blouse. You could see her curves from the front. Dudes stared at her, wishing they could taste the dark-skinned beauty. She looked totally different, like an American.

Za'alya hailed a cab to a hotel in Manhattan. This was her first time in New York and she was on a serious mission.

Weeks ago, Za'alya came back from Stockholm, Sweden after killing two Norwegian brothers to find her father dead and PYT gone. She knew PYT was in New York, or close, or at least someone knew where she was. She planned to start with the Empire.

Za'alya knew PYT had killed her father. She made it her first priority to see blood for his death.

She looked at the tall buildings and crowded streets filled with travelers. She liked the busy city. Lately she had been feeling sick and weak. She could also feel herself losing weight, so she planned to get a checkup first thing in the morning.

Once at her hotel, she planned out her events for the next day and called it a night. She could taste PYT's blood in her mouth.

Romell Tukes

Chapter 21

Agent Lopez was in a cheap motel with a Spanish woman he had met last week at a bike show upstate, which he went to every year. Lopez loved bikes. He had three bikes: a Harley Davidson, a 1961 Panhead, and an Indian Scout Bobber bike.

Things were going badly for him with his career and personal life. The Empire case was open and they were trying to piece everything together. When they find out he was the one covering the mess, he would be in a cell right next to them, but he refused to go out like that. He would give up his brother, mother, and sisters before he let the Feds put him under the jail. The walls were closing in and he didn't want to be a part of the bullshit when it all collapsed so he told his brother he was done.

The conversation with his brother didn't go too well at all, but Lopez was done. He had never been so scared until now because the top dogs in D.C. had picked the case up, which could be bad for everybody.

Lopez just got done fucking the young lady for forty minutes and she went to sleep. Her pussy and head game had him nutting left and right. She was easy, just like most young women who fell into his web, but at first she was playing hard to get until he broke her in.

She was a bad bitch with thick, long blond hair, Spanish features, and she looked like the model Tatted Up Holly with tattoos all over her ass and thighs.

Lopez felt his back hurting. He was getting old. He went to the bathroom to take a piss. He saw roaches and mice racing around the dirty bathroom floor. He took a piss, thinking about how crazy Gabby's head game was.

Lopez walked out of the bathroom wearing nothing with his brown dick hanging.

"Agent Lopez, how was the pussy? That was the least I could do for you," Red Hat said, pointing a gun at him as Yasmine stood there and Lyric got dressed.

Lyric was Gabby. She went to the bike show and he fell in her trap. When she was fucking him, she hated every minute of it, even after popping pills. Red Hat sent her on a mission and she did her part for the love of her life.

Lopez quietly recognized the man with the gun as Red Hat. He had only seen the man in photos until now and he knew he was in deep shit.

"Red Hat, come on, brother. I'm down with y'all. My brother won't be happy about this," Lopez said, ice grilling Lyric, mad at himself for letting a bitch set him up. He regretted licking her ass and sucking her toes. Now he wanted to kill the bitch.

"Lopez, your brother is the reason why I'm here. He told Rugar to X you out, so I'm here to handle that, fam. Sorry. Plus we got more agents on the payroll now: Patterson, Wilson, Howard, and Johnson," Red Hat said.

"Them dirtbags."

"Just like you."

Bloc! Bloc! Bloc! Bloc! Bloc!

Bullets riddled his body and he jerked until he hit the floor.

The three of them left the hotel, hoping they didn't have bedbugs, because the place was disgusting and smelled bad.

***

Miami, Fl.

Naya and PYT had just come from having a private lunch with their mom at a hotel.

Shah came to the States to see her kids and tell them the truth of why she played the background their whole lives. She told them how she was born into the Indian Cartel family, and about their other sister out there somewhere who might need their help.

PYT and Naya rode in the Bentley limo in silence, recounting everything they recently just heard.

"What do you think?" Naya asked her little sister.

"She saved my life. What else can I think? We not kids no more and we know her position because were both in positions ourselves," PYT said, looking out her window at the Miami nightlife.

"Facts. I'ma keep in touch with her. It's crazy because when she took off her hijab, she looked just like us, but younger" Naya said thinking how her mom looked when she removed her face wrap and her long silky hair dropped to the floor.

"Yeah, she is pretty. But I'ma go back home tonight after I spend more time with Brandon. I can't believe he was kidnapped too." PYT said.

"I know. I'm just glad he okay. He be training every day in the backyard. He really hurt about his teacher dying," Naya said, shaking her head

"I can't believe he killed all those people."

"Me neither, sis. I don't want him to be like us."

"He won't. At least I hope not," PYT said, praying for her nephew.

***

Staten Island

Big Smokey had to bury his mother today. He was sick. He had no clue who killed her or why. He just wanted revenge.

Today he just wanted to be alone. He was driving back home listening to Boys II Men, thinking about his mom.

When he finally made it home, he pulled into his four car garage with tears. As soon as he shut off his car, he felt a pistol to the back of his head. Someone had been in his backseat of his Wraith all day.

"Don't move," a female voice stated. "PYT...where is she?"

Big Smokey could hear the African accent in her tone.

"Who the fuck are you? PYT dead," he said.

"No, she's not. She is alive, and she is my sister," Za'alya stated.

Big Smokey had seen PYT weeks ago and he just Facetimed her two nights ago, venting about his mother's murder to her.

"Sorry, I can't help you, bitch." Big Smokey looked in his rearview mirror to see a dark-skinned sexy bitch with blond hair who could pass for a model.

"Okay. I'm sorry," she said, blowing his brains out all over his windshield. Then she escaped on foot.

Chapter 22
Miami, Lil Haiti

China was parked in a Walgreens parking lot in a gray Ford Focus with tints, watching civilians walk in and out of the store.

Her mind and thoughts had been fucked up since she lost the love of her life, Pressure. It took everything in her not to kill herself. She even tried swallowing a bottle of prescription pills.

China thought back to when the police told her Pressure was murdered. She passed out and when she woke up. She wished she was dead. She ended up having a miscarriage days later due to stress. That crushed her the most.

This was the second man she ever loved that was killed in the streets. King Cholo, who Lil C killed in New York when she was eighteen years old, was the first.

The night Pressure went to meet Jalee, he told China where he was going and who he was going to meet. The icing on the cake was that Pressure's phone pocket dialed her number, so she heard his and Jalee's whole conversation until he shot him and tossed him with the fishes.

China didn't tell the police shit. She was raised differently.

Today was the day Jalee would meet his fate. She had been trailing him for five hours while he was running errands in a white Lexus GS with tints.

Twenty minutes later he was pulling into a graveyard. The sky started to darken a little with an orange and purple skyline on the horizon.

China's mind started to race. She wondered why he was parking near Pressure's gravesite out of all places.

Within seconds, China saw him standing over Pressure's grave pissing on it, which made her cry as she watched him violate his grave.

***

Jalee was laughing while pissing on Pressure's grave. He was tipsy off the Henny. He was now focused on catching Romell slipping.

Since Pressure's murder, Jalee gave up the game and was focused on one thing: revenge. His wife was with him 100%, more than him.

After taking the piss, he placed his dick back in his Balmain jeans and turned around to come face to face with the barrel of China's pistol.

"You disrespectful bitch! I'ma make sure everyone you love pays for this shit," China stated with tears flowing down her face.

"Bitch, I'ma see you in hell," he said looking into her chinky eyes, seeing how beautiful his killer was.

Without even blinking, she shot him in the face four times and his body dropped in his own piss puddle.

China looked at her lover's grave and ran off into the night with a bite of happiness.

***

New York City

Naya was in New York to handle some personal business with the Empire that she just finished up an hour ago. She was on her way to the JFK airport to fly out to Atlanta to speak to one of Glizzy's security guards who had been at the club with

Glizzy, but had gone home after he went to the hotel with the white bitch. He reached out to Red Hat to tell him he had some reliable information about Glizzy's death, but since Red Hat was in D.C. on business, Naya was on her way out there.

Glizzy was new to the Empire, but he was a part of the family, and Naya believed in loyalty within the family. So whoever was responsible for his death would pay with their blood. She was on her way to the airport in an SUV with two more behind her full of her 24/7 personal security. Romell ordered that whenever she left without him, her license to kill guards be with her.

Since she came home, life had been full of blessings and downers, but overall, she always thanked Allah for blessing her.

**

Atlanta, GA

Naya was at a nice public restaurant in downtown Atlanta, waiting on Glizzy's guard, the one who was with him the night he was killed viciously.

Her guards were all over the small place, which was filled of black people enjoying good southern food: fried chicken, greens, rice, cabbage, and cornbread made from scrap.

Naya saw a big black ugly dude walk into the restaurant in a sweat suit, looking around as if he was lost. Naya had a feeling it was him, so she waved him over. When he saw her, he gladly approached her.

Big Toot was an ex-NFL player with a bad coke habit, which got him kicked out of the NFL for life and landed him a three year jail bid after he got caught with fifty grams in a

random traffic stop. Working for Glizzy paid the bills until he had been killed. Now he was homeless, living in a shelter.

"Hey," Naya said as he took a seat.

"What's up? Thanks for coming. Glizzy was family. I saw him grow into a man. He was holding a lot of nigga down out here in the A, including me. Now I have nothing, not even a pot to piss in," he said.

"He was a good dude, I agree."

"I know he was down with the Empire. Y'all name heavy out here. But this is why I reached out, because the night of the killing, I was recording some shit on my phone for Instagram for him and I caught a glimpse of the chick he was with," he said, showing her his phone and the video of Glizzy in the VIP with a beautiful white woman talking in what sounded like a French accent.

"You called me down here to show me that? Who doesn't have bitches in their VIP section? Shit, even I do when I go out," she said smartly.

"True, I understand that, but he went to the hotel with this woman."

"Okay, and...?"

"And my ex was there with her new man doing what they were doing and they saw Glizzy enter the hotel with the woman. Then hours later they saw her running out and hopping into a truck full of big white boys with baldheads who looked like Nazis," he said as she paused.

"Are you sure?"

"Yes, I am. Something isn't right about this. Nobody would just kill Glizzy. He was a very powerful man in the city." he said.

A'ight, look, send me the video and I'ma take care of it," she said, pulling out an envelope, setting it on the table before leaving.

Once she left, he opened the envelope to see $30,000.

***

Miami, FL

Later that night, Naya studied the video and showed it to Romell, asking him if he thought it was a hit or just a sex thing. When Romell saw the face and eyes, he knew it was Katie. He told her she was his connect and a part of the Cartel Commission, but he didn't tell her about their history. Naya was pissed. She couldn't believe that little bitch killed her family.

Romell Tukes

Chapter 23
Santiago de Cuba

PYT and Rugar were standing in their living room staring out their windows towards the backyard where the twenty-one Cartel families were all seated on this beautiful warm day. The Cartel Commission had started out with twenty-three international families plus Cuba and the USA, but now with Shota and Hubei murdered, that left twenty-one.

The past couple of weeks had been crazy for PYT, but she was trying to take it one day at a time. There was so much going on in her life. She didn't know whether to go left or right, but she was glad to have Rugar by her side.

"You sure you ready to reclaim your position within the Commission?" Rugar asked, fixing his suit, which was made by Ralph Lauren.

"I guess," she said, not too sure as she watched all the families talk amongst each other.

PYT wore a red Balmain corset style dress worth 32,000 with diamonds around her neck and wrist.

"You don't have to do this, Jasmine," he said, calling her by her real name.

"I know, but I chose this lifestyle just as much as it chose me, so it's no point in hiding from it," she said.

"A'ight. We stand strong together," Rugar stated, holding her hand, walking out the back of the house surrounded by guards and maids.

***

The cartel families were at their annual meeting, but none of them had a clue PYT was back, well and alive, except the Shah Family. They were seated at the end of the table quiet as

mice. Shah couldn't wait to see her daughter take her seat back.

Rugar and PYT walked out side by side towards the table. Everybody had shocked facial expressions.

"What the fuck?" the Costa Rica Cartel Family shouted in Spanish.

"Good afternoon, ladies and gentlemen, glad you could all make it again. Today is a special meeting because, as you see, my wife is back and doing well," he said.

Everybody started to clap as she took her seat.

"Thank you for all the help and connections trying to help me find my wife, especially Ms. Shah," Rugar said.

Everybody looked at the quiet lady who never talked and always had her face and body wrapped up.

"As you all see, two families are not here for a reason. The Shota Cartel family has been eliminated due to the kidnapping of my nephew," Rugar said. "Reason being because I killed his grandson years ago in a war in New York," he stated strongly.

"So we have a war within our own commission? Why weren't any of us notified? That's how shit normally worked over the past two decades," the Malaysia Cartel family head said, speaking up.

"I take full responsibility for that misunderstanding and my actions. I didn't want to disturb anyone unless it got out of hand," he said as everyone nodded.

"What happened to Hubei? He was a powerful businessman within the family and he could never do wrong in my eyes," the Libya Cartel family head stated with his Arabic accent, dressed like a mummy.

"Hubei was the one who kidnapped me and brought me to King Omen, who was my father, before he was murdered,"

PYT said. She saw a lot of awkward facial expressions as people were wary and shocked.

A lot of people had heard of King Omen, but they had no clue his daughter was a part of the commission. King Omen supplied most of South America with the purest opium poppy plants.

"I'ma make something clear with everyone in this room. We have twenty rules we all live by and follow until death, and one of them is sex trades and slaves. If we find out any one of you are having any dealings in the sex business, you will be dealt with," PYT said, looking at the Russia Cartel family head, who was breathing heavily.

"We have to tighten up and be more supportive with this cartel. We control the world's drugs and power," Rugar said, looking around.

"Since you mention this, what is the situation with the Empire in the States? We all know your connection, but I had to have my brother killed because your people are moving very sloppy," the Mexican Cartel family head stated.

Rugar had a feeling this would be brought up. He was just waiting for the perfect timing to address the situation.

"The Empire is a part of us, and I'm aware that they are being investigated by the government, but I can assure you they will not lead back to us in no type of way at any time," he said.

"I hope not," the Mexican Cartel head said, shaking his head, pissed off he even had dealings with black gang members.

"Now with my wife back, she will control the States, so I know things will be in order. But as far as business, does anybody have any issues?" he asked. Nobody said a word because they were all making millions off of the coke pills. "Okay, I guess we're done here."

After the meeting, there was a big dinner for the families to enjoy with all types of food: halal, Spanish food, and Caribbean food.

Shah and PYT talked in private upstairs in her room for over two hours until she caught her private jet flight back to India.

The cartel meeting was successful, but she had one person on her mind that she planned to visit very soon.

Chapter 24
Opa-Locka, Miami

Southside had just come from the club. He was driving through his hood in his 85 Dank, sitting on big rims with fish bowl tints and Gucci interior. A navy blue Tahoe truck was behind him, full of his young Haitian shooters holding the Dracos with extra clips. He was on his way to the projects where he was raised to meet up with his baby mother Sassy, who was a known sack chaser with a mean head game and some snap back pussy.

Pulling into the projects, he parked near his baby mother's apartment complex. There were over twenty-five apartment complexes in the largest projects in Opa-Locka.

Southside felt there was something off about tonight as he jumped out of his car. He wondered where everybody was because the projects were always live from morning to night.

"This shit ghost town, bruh-bruh," Paper Bay said, climbing out of the truck.

"Yeah. I'm about to go holla at Sassy. I'ma see y'all in the morning," Southside said, looking at all the clothes banging on the clotheslines in the backyard as he smelled the overloaded dumpster odor that contaminated the air.

"For sure," Paper Bay said.

He and four of his young boys were ambushed with flashlights and assault rifles by over forty Feds coming from abandoned cars in the lot, the dumpsters, the side of the buildings, and from the front of the projects, where seven vans were parked.

"Get down now!"

"Freeze!"

"Okay! Okay!" Paper Bay yelled as he was being tackled to the ground.

"He got a gun!" one of the agents yelled when they saw one of the young men pull out a 9mm with a 30 round on it.

The Feds lit his ass up with twenty-seven rounds, killing the sixteen-year-old boy.

Southside and his crew were tossed into the van, sick - not for Lil Rico's death, but because they all had felonies and somebody had to take the gun charges because they found four Dracos in the truck.

Once in the federal building, Southside saw sixty-two other niggas. Most of them he knew already, and the rest he didn't.

There was a sixty-four man indictment and he was number three.

Romell was number one and then Pressure was number two, but luckily he was already dead. When the Feds interrogated him, they showed him pictures of dead niggas he killed. Southside knew he was done so he wasted no time singing like Mary J. Blige in a concert. Southside snitched on Romell and forty other niggas that weren't on his indictment, but he knew with his help, another indictment was on its way.

He told the Feds everything they needed to know about Romell and he told on over thirteen murders he personally knew Romell did or had been the one to have them killed.

He was in the interrogation room for six hours then they placed him on P.C. because they knew how powerful Romell's reach was.

***

Guantanamo, Cuba

Rugar was asleep in his small mansion where he normally came to relax and clear his mind.

PYT was in New York with Naya and the Empire, getting the shipments in order. She was on her shit back and forth to the States and Cuba.

Shit was going well, but he could tell there were still a lot of personal issues within the Commission. But that was little. He made a mental note to check that shit at the next year's meeting.

Rugar slept with the balcony door open every night because he loved the Cuban warm breezy air. It helped him sleep, unlike the New York December weather that would give you the flu the next morning.

He was knocked out until he heard the sound of a moving curtain, but the noise was like a blanket dropping in the air on the floor. Rugar looked to his left to see nothing except moving drapes due to the breeze from outside. Seeing it was nothing, Rugar turned back around to feel a sharp pressure to his neck from a bloody sword

"Don't fucking move. Where is Zeema?" a female voice stated aggressively.

"I don't know, but you're making a big mistake, Za'alya," he said already knowing who it was from her accent. PYT told him the whole story, so he knew it could only be her.

Za'alya killed all ten of his guards downstairs and outside. Most of them were asleep, which made it easy blood for her sword.

"She killed my father. I kill you," she said.

Rugar couldn't even look her in her eyes because she was behind him, but he could smell her strong African black soap scent.

"You're dead whether you kill me or not."

"I'm already dead, I contracted HIV in my country," she said with tears. She had gone for a checkup yesterday to find out she had HIV. She didn't want to believe it, but she knew

she had to live with it like 65% of people in her country. "I'm sure this will send her a message" Za'alya said, cutting his neck open with a swift swing of her sword. Blood poured out his neck like a waterfall.

Za'alya was about to finish the job until she saw a young pretty Spanish woman dressed in an army camouflage uniform run in the room shooting.

Za'alya clocked the bullets, diving on the other side of the bed, and a bullet glazed her shoulder.

"Fuck." Za'alya didn't like guns. She was a fighter and sword fighter.

Savannah was shooting up the room, hitting up everything in the room except Za'alya. Savannah was stalking Rugar and when she saw Za'alya run in his crib, she followed suit to see a trial of bodies lying around the house.

Savannah looked on the bed for the first time to see Rugar laying there slumped dead in his pool of blood.

Savannah was pissed. She ran to the other side of the bed to see Za'alya gone already. There was no way she could get away that fast with her standing there.

She looked out the open balcony, then figured out how she escaped. Savannah looked back at Rugar and cried for the first time in a long time.

She hated herself for not getting there sooner. She saw his head hanging off his neck like a stuffed doll. Savannah left the house in an emotional state. She never thought Rugar would get killed. Out of all people on earth, why him?

Chapter 25
New York City
FBI Station 6

Agent Berkeley and Captain Raymond from the New Jersey FBI headquarters both sat in Berkeley's skyrise office.

"I'm so glad we can finally work together," said Agent Berkeley, who was leaning back in his recliner chair.

"Same here. I've been in this force a long time and it's rare to come across good agents as yourself," Captain Raymond replied, lying through his teeth. He had never heard of Berkeley until he heard about the Empire being investigated.

Since he killed Froster, who Twin sent at him, he hadn't been able to sleep at night because all he wondered about was who he would send next to finish the job. If it wasn't for his lovely wife, he would have been dead. He thanked her every day.

"Since Lopez's death I've been coming across a lot of links to a lot of heavy hitters, but it's like he was keeping shit a secret," Agent Berkeley stated with a crazy look as he logged into his computer.

"What do you mean?" Captain Raymond asked. He always had a funny feeling Lopez was up to no good.

"For starters, he had photos of a man who is the so-called leader of the Mexican Cartel. I believe they call him Joseph or something," he said.

"Ain't that some shit! What else you got?"

"I got a female connected to these Empire hoodlums named Naya, but I don't know her connection. I just got her on a few wiretaps, but she's not really saying much. I sense they have a lot of respect for her. Maybe because she just came home from prison." Agent Berkeley said, shrugging his frail shoulders.

Captain Raymond felt his blood rush. He could tell Berkeley wasn't that bright. Naya had history. He was the first person to investigate her for murders of rival Crips in a vicious gang war in Newark, NJ years ago.

"My ex-partner is the one who arrested her years ago - before he retired, I should say - but she ended up giving her time back, which shook the hell outta me," he said.

"Did you know she got married to a guy named Romell who was recently indicted on all types of murders and 848 RICO laws and all types of shit?" Agent Berkeley said reading it off a computer.

"They caught him?"

"Nope, he is a fugitive," Berkeley stated.

"So they're married, huh? How the fuck did two fucking drug lords meet at a fucking stop and shop," Captain Raymond stated, trying to piece shit together.

I don't know, but it's weird. We're missing a lot of pieces to this puzzle. What we need is an insider or someone close who can fill us in on what's really what," Berkeley stated as Captain Raymond nodded.

Captain Raymond thought this was brilliant. He had the right person in mind, but it was very risky and he knew if he saw him before the Feds did, he vowed to kill him.

"I have something in mind," Raymond said, catching his attention.

"What's that?"

"You have warrants and indictments out for everyone in the Empire?"

"I believe so. Bullet, Red Hat, Big Smokey and Twin, then eighty-six street soldiers," he said.

"Okay, since Twin is the one who tried to kill me, we going to charge him with attempted murder on a federal officer. That alone holds 100 years. That will break him. Trust

me, he's nothing like his twin brother Mark. He was the heart and muscle," Raymond said.

"Okay, I'll do the warrant now."

"Do that. I'll have it signed by a judge first thing in the morning," Raymond said, smiling.

"Hopefully he will lead us to bigger fish," Berkeley said, texting someone.

"Fish? This guy's going to lead us to the sharks," Raymond said, laughing.

***

Bhopal, India

Anna Shah rode in the backseat of a bulletproof all-black Ford truck with two behind her, on her way home from a long day of shopping. She loved shopping. That was her thing besides meditating and exercising, doing yoga, plus swimming in her backyard pool.

Lately she had been back and forth to the States, checking on Naya and PYT while building a bond with them both. It always hurt her to be out of her children's lives for so long but she had to or their lives would have been short-lived because she had a lot of enemies.

Anna wanted to build a solid relationship with her children because she had breast cancer. It was new to her. She found out months ago from her own personal doctor.

She still hadn't told her daughters yet because she hadn't found the right time to really present it.

There was something else she needed to find out and she wanted to find her other daughter before it was too late.

Her doctor told her she had less than one year to live, if that, and she made it her number one goal to find her other daughter. She could be anywhere.

Anna was lonely - no husband and no life. She never wanted to die like this, but she was willing to accept her fate.

She looked out her window to see all the poor families living out of boxes in alleys, dirty, striving, and sick with all types of diseases. She wished she could help the world, but she was only one person. She had already opened six schools, homes, stores, and shelters.

***

An hour later

Ivanovich was in his office chair watching the redhead go to work. She was bopping her head up and down on his dick, fucking him down her throat.

"Ummm…" he moaned as she made a loud slurping noise while twisting her head on the top of his dick.

She was sucking all the pre-cum out of his dick as she sped up. He felt her body warm up as her pussy got extra wet. She was now feeling the effect from the heroin. All she wanted to do was suck his dick until her jaws locked. She never thought she was a freak.

Gunfire could be heard downstairs, which snapped him out of his zone. He pushed the red head and stood up to pull up his pants. Before his pants were on his waist, a gun slapped him across his head, knocking him on the floor.

"What the fuck?" he said feeling his head. Blood was leaking from it. He looked up to see PYT standing there.

"Surprise," she said looking at the frail redhead little girl. "Go downstairs," she told her, looking into her drowsy eyes. She could tell she was high off of something.

The girl ran downstairs with her little ass cheeks bouncing.

PYT had been hiding in his office closet for six hours. She saw the whole oral sex scene, which made her sick. She was waiting for her team to enter the front and back to kill all the guards. She had been waiting on this day for years.

"Why are you here? You are violating a lot of the rules," he said as if he was innocent.

"Really? Don't remember me, do you?" she said.

"No, besides being Rugar's wife."

"I'm King Omen's daughter." she said.

The name sounded familiar, but didn't click

"Does Za'alya ring a bell? Years ago I was the girl in the cage you wanted to buy, but she refused to sell me so you took Jolien and Amber instead," she said.

"Oh shit..." he said, now remembering exactly who she was and knowing he was caught red-handed.

"Yeah, I'm sure you remember now," she said pointing her gun at his face. He looked scared to death.

"Please, I'm sorry."

"Don't do that. Where are the two girls and the little kids that were in the cage with me that day?"

"The kids were re-sold to some rich family in Miquelon and one of the girls overdosed off drugs months ago. The Amber girl is in my master bedroom."

`After he said that, she emptied her seventeen shot clip in his body, then exited to find Amber.

Seconds later, she walked into his bedroom, which was very large, and saw five young girls hiding on the side of the bed. She saw Amber first and told them they were now free and safe.

Amber remembered PYT's face from three years ago and hugged her tightly with her naked body, crying. She hated herself in life. She was forced to have sex, do drugs, fuck six to nine guys at once, and more crazy shit that her young body couldn't handle.

PYT brought all the girls with her downstairs to see twenty-two other girls lined up with her sixteen guards. Dead bodies could be seen everywhere, even on steps.

They all left the caste sitting on top of a hill in the mountains on their way to Moscow to free the women and help whoever they could.

***

Black Mist retired from the killing game and now he was traveling and living life he had dreamed of for years. He was living outside of the Sahara in a tent within a small city. He woke up next to a dark-skinned woman dressed in an Islamic garment with her face wrapped in a hijab.

Last night he was out drinking and met her and they kicked it off, then one then led to another they were having sex all night in his large dark tent that was the size of a small house.

Black Mist never had pussy as good as he had last night and her head game was official. He was so drunk he didn't even catch her name. He just remembered her hazel eyes and phat ass that was bouncing up and down on his dick. He was old, but he still fucked like a young nigga in his twenties.

Black Mist went to take a piss. He felt his dick burning. He hoped it wasn't what he was thinking.

Before he could even finish, he felt a sharp pain enter his back and side. He turned around to see the woman stabbing him. He tried to fight her, but he had already lost too much blood so he was weak. He felt the sword rip through his heart that dropped him as Za'alya continued to stab him again and again.

She had been hunting for Black Mist for weeks because she heard he was in Zimbabwe the day Omen was murdered and she knew the serious beef they had. She had an idea he could have killed her pops because she didn't think PYT was that skillful. She followed him to Mauritania, a Muslim country, and caught him drunk and fucked him good, falling into his trap.

Now she could go back hunting for Zeema.

Chapter 27
Miami, Fl.

Romell was riding in a bulletproof Ghost Rolls Royce with a Hummer full of Haitian hitters behind him.

Shit had been crazy lately for him with this big federal indictment that snatched up most of his men. Rugar's death was big. Everybody was crushed this time.

With Naya back and forth to New York dealing with the Empire and spending quality time with her son, they had little time with each other unless it was sleeping at night.

He was on his way to meet with one of his buyers in downtown Miami. He wanted to see all the evidence the Feds had on him. There were twenty-fight niggas on his indictment telling on him and come to find out Southside was number one.

Southside knew so much shit about Romell. He could go back to when he was fourteen putting in work because the two were from the same projects in Dade County.

Romell looked out the tints, thinking it would be best to get out of the States with his family for a little while. He still hadn't told Naya about him being a wanted man, but he did bring up the fact that he wanted to move.

He had been at his mini mansion in Coconut Grove since his indictment dropped, but luckily he had nothing in his name except a bank account at Chase bank with $120 in it. One thing about the Feds: they will seize everything you have if it's under your name, so he was two steps ahead of them.

Lil Brandon was back in private school. He just celebrated his fourteenth birthday. He was still practicing martial arts and living a teenage life.

Romell was a block away from Thomas Park where his lawyer Mrs. Grace was awaiting him to tell him what was going on.

As he stopped at a red light, he saw an all-black Mustang pull up next to him with tints with the window half-cracked. The light turned green and the Mustang swerved in front of the Ghost, cutting it off. Before Romell could even say anything, a woman who looked familiar hopped out, shooting a MP assault rifle. Once she saw the high-powered rifle was doing nothing to the Ghost, she turned the Hummer to Swiss cheese, killing everyone inside.

Joggers and other drivers saw what was going on and quickly reversed, going the opposite direction.

Romell grabbed his Draco and hopped out, shooting, hitting the shooter in her leg as she took off. She hopped in the Mustang, burning rubber as bullets busted out her windows and tail lights.

Romell saw police lights two blocks away down the long narrow streets. He climbed in the back of the Ghost as his driver made a quick right, then did 70 mph until he saw an intersection leading on to the expressway.

Romell was pissed. The woman's face came clearly to him now. It was Jalee's girlfriend, the bad bitch who he brought to the club the first time he met him. He vowed to find that little bitch, whoever she really was. She was on a mission. He felt something off about her when he first laid eyes on her.

***

New York

Savannah had on sunglasses with her hair in a ponytail, wearing tight jeans and a LV Supreme top and high heels,

walking through the airport. Savannah looked like a real Puerto Rican chick from the Bronx.

Since Rugar's death, she had been mentally unstable. She felt like she was the one married to Rugar instead of PYT.

Weeks ago she was creeping on Rugar's Cuba real estate to see a beautiful woman taking a swim with a body ten times better than hers. She became so jealous she was ready to kill her, but when she saw Rugar come outside and the woman climbed out of the pool, she saw that it was PYT. She couldn't get the image of Rugar laying in his bed dead with his neck sliced open like a pig's stomach out of her head.

Savannah did her research on the female assassin she saw that night and her connection to Rugar and it all led back to PYT.

Savannah had connections in a lot of countries thanks to her mother, whom she hated. She wished she was the one who killed her instead of PYT.

It was winter time in New York, so she was frozen. She was so used to Cuba's tropical weather. This cold shit was new to her.

Savannah had a feeling Za'alya had to be on her heels in either NY or Miami.

Since Rugar's death, it was as if PYT got ghost again. If she could find her, she could kill two birds with one stone.

She climbed in an Uber that pulled up and made her way to the Bronx, seeing snow for the first time.

***

Lima, Peru

PYT was sitting on the beach behind her beach house sticking her toes in the white sand, crying as she had been

doing for a week now since Rugar's death. His death shocked her and what made it so crazy was she was the first person to find him there slumped on his damp red bloody sheets.

She felt lost and empty without Rugar. He was her life. He was the reason she was so strong and militant minded.

There was only one person who could have done this and that was her sister. She knew sooner or later they would meet because she vowed to get revenge for his death by any means.

She looked into the crystal clear water. She needed to clear her mind because there was still the Cartel Commission she needed to run since Rugar's only next of kin was Brandon or China, and neither one was cut for this type of life. She lost a lot with in a matter of years but she also gained family, friends, and more power.

***

Dade County Jail

Southside was on the phone in the dayroom on the PC block filled with snitches, rapists, and inmates too scared to go to general population. He was on the phone yelling at one of his baby mothers about child support and who was going to take care of his kids now.

Since telling on Romell, he felt bad because he knew him and Pressure since the sandbox, but he had to save himself. He was facing a life sentence if he didn't rat. Now he was facing 30 years, the minimum, after he took the stand on Romell.

"Bitch, I'm not giving you shit, believe that!" he yelled.

Two new inmates walked in the dayroom with bed rolls and he paid them no mind.

Southside was so caught up in yelling into the phone he didn't even see one of the inmates pull out an eight inch

homemade knife and attack him. The men stabbed Southside in the neck, face, head, and upper torso until the turtles came with shields and pepper spray, fucking everybody up in their way.

By the time they made it to Southside, he was dead after being stabbed forty-seven times. Thanks to Romell's reach and $100,000, the main witness was out of the picture.

The men came from population, but one of them told a correctional officer he couldn't live on his unit because he owed money and was scared for his life, so they had to move him to PC (protected custody).

When they moved him, he was plotting his move. With 100,000 on Southside's head, he was going to get it. He was already sentenced to 225 years. Another body wouldn't hurt the man.

Romell Tukes

Chapter 28
New York City
7:30 p.m.

Naya looked around the conference room in one of PYT's accountant firms she wanted to use for the Empire meeting. Everybody in the room was wanted by the Feds. She had many inside workers in the Bureau so she always made sure she was two steps ahead for her crew - not her, because she wasn't on the indictment.

She looked at Twin, Red Hat, and Bullet. Everybody else was now a memory. Never in a million years would she have thought they would lose Brazy, Bam Bam, Glizzy, and the funniest nigga she ever met, Big Smokey. But losing Rugar hurt the worst for some reason. She saw him grow up and she basically gave him the game after his brother died.

Naya wore a red Prada dress with a red mink hanging from her shoulders because winter time was like the North Pole.

A couple of days ago, Romell had a shootout in Miami. She felt like everything was going badly. She even sent her son with a close friend of Romell who lived a square life with his family because she was scared shit was about to get nasty and Romell was a wanted man.

"To be honest, I don't know what to say no more. This Empire was built ground up with all of our blood, sweat and tears," she said.

"Facts," Bullet stated in his tailor made Dior for men suit.

"Never in a million years could I regret anything I've done in life. Y'all help made me who I am today. It's not even about the money because we believe in loyalty before royalty, but it's about the love we have for each other and the Bloods on the East Coast," she said.

"Talk that shit, son," Red Had said, smiling in a Celine sweater and pants.

"We all lived a good life," Twin said, being honest, feeling as if he did everything anyone could dream of.

"You right. But there must be an end to every short-lived dream, and gentlemen, this is it." She looked around to see sad faces. "The Feds want everybody in this room except me because I just came home and I was off the radar. Tonight they will be raiding everyone's homes, businesses, and family homes."

"This shit fucked up," Twin said, pissed.

"It's the game," Red Hat stated.

"I have a new identity for you all: new bank accounts, and new location for each of you," she said passing around three folders with passports, ID's, PIN numbers, addresses, and photos of someone who was similar to them

Red Hat was the first to open his folder. "Raugar Docks in Oslo, Norway," said Red Hat, stating his new location and life as a truck driver.

"Kampala, Uganda," said Twin, saying his new residence as a doctor in Uganda.

"Asmara, Eritrea. Where the fuck is that at? And I will be working as a food stand worker," Bullet stated, pissed off.

"Yes, this will be your new life until I find a way to clear you all out the Feds' limelight. Rugar is dead; PYT is God knows where. I can't let none of you go down and this is the only way."

"Fuck that shit," Twin said, slamming his fist on the table, getting up to walk out, leaving the meeting.

"He'll be okay, but this is it. Our last Empire meeting. So farewell. I love y'all. I will be doing everything in my power to clear you all and find Rugar's killer, but until then, please follow the rules so we can still be able to live a fancy

lifestyle," she said, referring to the money in their off-shore accounts, which was close to a billion apiece.

"I guess. Until next time," Red Hat said as he stood up and gave Naya a hug and Bullet some dap.

Everybody went their separate ways with a ton of heavy thoughts on their minds.

***

8 months later
Miami, FL

PYT was sitting in a coffee shop on South Beach Boulevard wearing Chanel sunglasses and a female Dolce and Gabbana suit with a Rolex Rugar had given to her years ago.

She had been back in the States for three weeks and she was back like she never left - same house, same guards,

Since Rugar was dead, his next of kin in his bloodline had to take his seat within the Cartel Commission and since Brandon was underage, there was no way he could take that position. Today she was here to meet China. Since she was the next of kin, she wanted to try to talk her into taking the head seat amongst the families. This was her first time seeing China since Rugar had his closed casket funeral a while back, which she hated thinking about.

When she saw China approaching her table in an all-white Versace with the shades covering her chinky eyes, she smiled, glad to see her sister-in-law.

"Hey." The two embraced. China was glad to see her.

"How you been? You look amazing," China told her.

"Same to you," PYT said, looking at the girl's curves busting out of her dress.

"It's been a while. Where was ya at?" China asked.

"Overseas, then I was spending time with my mom in India. I had to regroup and rebuild myself," she stated, drinking a hot cup of herbal tea.

"I feel you. Since Pressure died and then Rugar ninety days later after him, my mind has been fucked up. I can't lie, Jasmine, there isn't a night where I don't think about them," she said, emotional.

"We gotta be strong because we're the last of the bloodline. But I called you here for something else." PYT took off her shades, looking around to see her guard near the exit reading newspapers and drinking coffee.

"What might that be?" China said, taking off her shades.

PYT saw something in her eyes. It was the look of death and pain. "I need you to take your brother's position with the head of the Cartel families. China, you are the only one who can fully take his throne since Hagar's daughter is God knows where and Brandon is too young. Your family legacy is in your hands."

China was silent. "I understand," was her only reply.

"You don't have to do nothing except lay back and be the boss bitch you already are. You understand?" PYT questioned her.

"Yes. I will do it," she said softly as if she had it figured out.

"Are you sure?"

"Jasmine, I may be pretty, a school girl, quiet, but I watched my family run the streets for years. It's all I know. It's all about being a mastermind. The thing that I have that my brothers didn't is patience," China said, being honest, because all her brothers were always impatient and even PYT knew that.

"You're correct. I'ma prepare the next meet and greet, but just know you're about to embark on a whole 'nother lifestyle," PYT said before getting up to leave.

Romell Tukes

Chapter 29
Bristol, U.K.

Romell was shoving his massive dick inside of Katie's warm tight pussy as if he had a point to prove and a reputation to live up to. Romell's eyes were wide open as if he was in another zone as he pounded her pussy out and she yelled, moaned and screamed.

Katie had slipped a powerful ecstasy pill in his drink hours ago and seduced him, then one thing led to another in the bedroom of her 8,176 square feet mansion on a lake border.

Shocked at how deep he was going, she was screaming out in sexual pleasure as he went in and out of her while her pussy muscles gripped his dick so tight he almost gave out. Romell's thrusts and strokes made an impact on Katie's small petite body every time he pounded on top of her.

"Uhhh...uhhh, shit, daddy," she said, feeling like she was ready to explode in pure bliss. She grabbed the pillow near her head, trying to cover her loud screams and avoid Romell seeing her face.

"You gave up yet?" he shouted in a cocky, arrogant manner as they switched positions. He made her bend over.

"Fuck no," she moaned as he rammed his dick in the wetness from behind, smacking her round, soft, perfect ass.

Romell was fucking her crazy as her body continued to orgasm. She felt her body go into shock. Katie was ready to throw in the towel, but she couldn't. It felt so good feeling his big dick kill her guts.

"Give up. You know you can't take this dick," he gritted, feeling the full effect of the ecstasy getting the best of him.

"Shut the fuck up and fuck me!" she screamed, catching another orgasm.

Romell nutted in her, not even realizing it until his dick softened inside of her, and then they both collapsed on the soaked sheets.

Katie felt guilty for drugging him, but it was all worth it to her. She loved his dick game and it was the only way she was going to get some.

Since Romell moved into her guest house last week, she had been plotting on how to get some dick and tonight was the night.

Romell was on the run from the Feds and he figured he would be well-protected by the cartel family who ran the UK.

Once everything started to come back to regular for him, her looked at Katie to see her naked and standing on a tab on an eBook reading an urban novel from her favorite book company, Lockdown Publications.

"You fucking drugged me, you crazy bitch!" Romell shouted.

"Romell, shut up, it's not that serious, especially the way you was eating my phat pussy. You shouldn't have nothing to say," she said with a chuckle.

Romell checked her up, raising her off the bed, almost killing her

"Bitch, if you ever pull some shit like that again while I'm alive, I'll kill you, do you hear me?" he said, choking the life out of her on the wall while her face turned beet red.

Katie nodded her head. If it was anybody else that put their hands on her, she would have killed their whole family. She picked herself up from the floor rubbing her neck. "I'm sorry," she said with her London accent as she got dressed in a Gucci rope with matching slippers.

"Whatever," he said, getting dressed, ready to go to his guest house on the side of the house. But first he had to get past the seventy guards all over the house, who were nosy.

He couldn't lie to himself. He knew what was going on when he was fucking Katie, but he was so horny and the pussy was so good he had to tear it up.

"I have something I wanted to show you for years, I'm twenty-seven now. I remember when I met you eight years ago," she said, smiling.

He followed her out of her room into a small door that looked like a closet next to her room on the second floor of her home.

"Where we going? I have no time for your games tonight," he stated seriously, already tired.

"Shhh..." she said, looking back at him, walking into the room. It was large with kid toys, walls, clothes everywhere. It looked like a small daycare center.

Katie walked over to the bed to where a light-skinned kid was asleep. He had good hair, good skin, almond-shaped blue eyes, high cheekbones, and thick eyebrows. Romell couldn't help but wonder why the little boy under the covers with his face sticking out looked like he could be his little brother.

"Who this, your little brother?" Romell asked.

"No."

"Nephew?"

"No, he's our son," she said catching him off-guard.

"Ain't no way, Katie. I don't know what types of games you playing, but it can't be," he said.

"Romell, it's okay, I don't need your help and I'm not trying to trap you. But he is yours. The first time we had sex, years ago I became pregnant," she said honestly.

"That was only one time."

"That's all you need, Romell. Here, read this," she said, walking to the closet to grab some paper while the little kid was asleep peacefully.

Romell couldn't lie. The kid looked just like a light-skinned version of him. "Damn, Katie, why wait so long to tell me if it's true?" he said as she was digging out some papers in the closet.

"Here you go. I wanted to wait because you went to jail and when you came home, you were busy building your own Empire. I run a Cartel, so I can understand the pressure and time you needed to get your life in order, then you got married. Now you have your own family, so it was never good timing," she said handing him DNA test results as he began to read.

"Wait, how the fuck did you get my DNA?"

"A while back when I was at your condo, I took some shit out your crib and submitted it, and as you see, it was a 99.9% match," she said as he read it, shaking his head, not mad but shocked he was really a father.

"Mommy…" the little kid said, turning in his sleep with his eyes closed.

"Yes, baby, go to sleep. Mommy just checking on you," she said, tucking him, in telling Romell to get out with her hands. But he didn't.

He was at a loss for words. He had a baby with a crazy white bitch who was rich and ran a powerful cartel. Romell knew he had to keep this secret from Naya until the time was right because this could end their love.

Once they stepped out of the room, Romell laid down the law. He told her she was his baby mother and he would be in his child's life regardless. She agreed and was happy. Even though he was married and wanted by the Feds, she was just glad to have him in her life.

The two went to sleep in the same bed without any sexual activity.

166

Chapter 30
Santiago de Cuba, Cuba

All twenty-one cartel families were seated at the long table in the backyard of PYT's mansion, which Rugar left her.

Today was a long day for the Cartel Commission because Rugar's seat would have to be filled.

"This is the first meeting since the loss of my husband," PYT said with a pause, because it was still hard to mention his name without getting emotional.

"We understand," said Costilla from the Columbia Cartel family. She looked beautiful in her yellow sundress with a rose stuck in her bun. Her looks could fool anybody, but she was a cold-blooded killer.

"Thanks, but as we all know, someone has to fill his seat and run the commission. There are only two options and one isn't suitable but the one who is should be on her way out any minute," PYT said, looking behind her to see China walking out the back door.

All eyes were on China. She was wearing a red Alexander McQueen tight mini skirt dress with her curves poking out and her DD breasts sitting up with her pierced nipples poking out of her dress. She was eye candy to every man in the room. Her hazel chinky Korean eyes and long jet black silky hair would corrupt the preacher if he saw her coming to church like this.

"What the fuck is this, *America's Next Top Model*?" the leader of the Mexican Cartel stated, knowing a woman couldn't run a Cartel Commission.

"This is China, Rugar's blood sister, and today she is here to take her brother's throne. It's twenty-one votes in here today plus, and mine makes twenty-two," PYT said as China was standing and looking around.

"I know what you all are thinking, but please don't get it fucked up. I'm just a cold as everyone in this room, if not colder. I will carry on my family torch, supply the best bricks, pills, dope, and oil money can buy. I'm not a regular person. If crossed, you will be dead. One mistake will cost you your life and good business will make us all trillionaires," China said. Most families could tell she had Jumbo and Rugar's bloodline.

"With that being said let's make the vote," PYT said as she was the first to lift her glass fill of Dom P, which meant she voted her in.

Glasses started to go in the air back to back. Katie and Costilla weren't playing. They both stood with their glasses, happy to see a woman in power instead of a man.

"Damn," PYT said as she saw two glasses on the table, which was the Mexican Cartel leader Joseph and Mr. Babanov, who was best friends with Mr. Hubei from the China Cartel family before PYT killed him.

"Well, it looks like I'm here to stay. I swore myself into the Commission oath already so with that being said, we have two issues at hand and I would like to clear the air," she said with a smile.

"China, what's wrong?" PYT asked, seeing a weird look on her face.

"Yeah," China stated, pulling out a big 40 caliber pistol and shooting Joseph in the head and then Mr. Babanov, getting blood on a couple of the family members. They were shocked, never seeing this before.

"China, what the fuck have you done?" PYT asked, knowing China just started a big war within the Cartel Commission.

"Let me explain. I'm sorry for the blood, but Joseph violated rule 8 and Babanov violated rule 9. Joseph had his

brother killed, the FBI agent, but before that, he forced him to build a case on the Costilla Cartel family because she wouldn't sleep with him," China said, playing a wiretap of Joseph telling his brother to investigate Costilla because she was a rich stuck up bitch and he told him to throw her under the jail with his connections.

When Costilla heard this shit, she was pissed. She wished she would have been the one who killed the creep.

"This is crazy," the Fiji Cartel family head said.

"As far as Mr. Babanov, you can all watch this," China said pissing around her large phone, showing a video of a Kyrgyzstani woman tied up speaking in Kyrgyz. The woman was saying she was a paid assassin paid to kill PYT for Babanov, who wanted her dead. She then said she was told to kill her slowly the same way she did Hubei.

Once everybody saw the video they were shocked, especially when they saw China kill her execution style with six shots to the back of her head.

PYT was pissed. She could have got caught slipping by someone in her own circle. She had no clue China was this crazy and official.

"I'm sure that's justice done until next time," she said, walking off, smiling, leaving all of them fucked up in the head, wondering what they just signed up for.

***

New York, BX

Red Hat was in the driver's seat of his black Bentley speeding, through the Soundview streets of the Bronx, about to go to the JFK airport with Yasmine and Lyric with him.

"Baby, I'm so happy to leave the States," Yasmine said with her new false ID and passport.

"Me too," Lyric said from the back seat, fixing her make-up.

Red Hat was listening to an old LOX album as he was driving across a bridge over a lake. A black van was speeding up behind him but didn't second guess who it was.

"Fuck, we got company," Red Hat said, speeding down the long narrow bridge to see a plumbing van cutting him off, slowing him down. He felt his tires being shot out as he swerved into a rail, crashing

"Damn!" he yelled as two vans blocked him in and federal agents started to hop out.

"I love y'all," he said as Lyric and Yasmine grabbed an SK and AR 15 then hopped out busting, killing two agents off.

Red Hat was shooting his Draco, taking chunks out of the van as another one pulled up.

Lyric was shooting it out like Queen Latifah in *Set It Off* while Yasmine was ducking from the crazy gunfire. More cars kept pulling up with agents. Now there were over twenty-five agents there.

One of the agents caught three to the head from the Draco as the women tried to cover him while shooting it out. Lyric's rifle jammed and before she could even fix it, ten bullets rippled her upper body as she fell in Yasmine's arms.

Dammit!" Red Hat yelled, now busting like a madman.

Yasmine dived over a couple of cars, taking out six agents, Red Hat yelled for her to stop and take cover, but she was in her feelings about Lyric.

It wasn't long before they placed thirty rounds in her thick body, killing her on the bridge, which was now flooded with dead bodies and agents.

Red Hat knew he wasn't making it out alive so he looked behind him to see the Hudson River as bullets tore through his Bentley, barely missing him.

Red Hat dashed towards the rail as bullets bounced off the rail and ground. He dived over the rail into the water head first, like the true swimmer he was in middle and high school.

Chapter 31
Patterson, New Jersey

Twin was leaving a neighborhood called Downhill filled with Bloods. Most of them he did jail time with or he was their supplier. Tonight he was leaving the States. He had rented a private jet for the first time in his life.

Since the indictment, he had been low key and out of Newark, NJ. He couldn't go back to jail. He had too much to risk. For one, he had his five-year-old daughter he had to raise correctly. He was mad he let himself come home off on appeal and get right back into the shit that got him in jail, but on a bigger level.

He was on his way to his child's mother's house. Quanny was a brown-skinned beautiful curvy woman in her early 30's who owned a daycare center.

Today was a rainy day, so the roads were wet and slippery as he pushed his baby mother's Honda Civic through the main streets.

Pulling into his baby mother's apartment complex parking lot, he saw it was full, which never happened, especially at 3 p.m. in the afternoon because most of the residents had 9 to 5 jobs. Luckily he saw a Ford Escape pulling out of a parking spot. The old lady almost hit his bumper.

He pulled right in the spot once she pulled out. He squeezed between two new-looking GMC trucks with New York license plates, which was odd to him but he thought his paranoia was getting the best of him.

Twin wanted to spend some time with his baby mother and fuck her because he knew it was going to be a long time before he'd see her again.

As soon as he opened his car door, he was ambushed by forty something agents. They even climbed in the car and were wrestling with him until they got him in cuffs.

The Feds found two AK-47s in the backseat and a Mack 11 in the passenger seat. That was just a couple of more counts to add to his indictment.

When they were hauling him off, Quanny and the five-year-old daughter ran downstairs, trying to stop them from taking him away, but it didn't stop the agents from pulling off with Twin. He looked at them from behind the tints of a GMC truck.

***

Newark, NJ

Twin was sitting quietly in the dim interrogation room getting ice grilled by Captain Raymond and two other agents who were ready to jump on his ass at any given moment.

"Marky Mark!" Cap Raymond laughed, walking back and forth with his hands behind his back.

"Fuck you, pig," Twin said while Raymond rushed him and slapped blood out of his mouth.

"No, fuck you, motherfucker! I could have been dead if it wasn't for my wife. You tried to kill me. I'll make sure the judge throw the book at you, nigga," Raymond said with flames.

"You will be someone's jailhouse bitch," one of the agents said with a laugh.

"I'ma give you something, a chance to save yourself, even though I shouldn't give you shit except a bunk in a cell," Raymond said.

"The only thing you can give me is your wife's pussy to suck, bitch-ass nigga!"

"You got a fresh mouth on you, boy. Let's see how big it is when big Bubba rams his big dick in there," Raymond said, making everyone laugh

"What you got for me, pig?" Twin said.

"A chance to get out of jail. I'll put to the side how you tried to kill me for now, but help us and you'll be a free man or get less than three years in a camp somewhere fucking C.O. bitches in the wood on weekends.

"I'm not a rat."

"You will be if you want to get out of this. I'll give you thirty minutes. You got twenty-nine left," he said, walking out with the two white agents behind him.

Twin's mind was racing. He had so much to lose, and he didn't want to die in jail like most of his homies doing time. He knew he had to make a big choice quickly.

Raymond walked back in the room alone with a stack of papers, smiling from ear to ear

"Where do you want me to start? This is going to be long," Twin said, ready to sing.

Raymond pulled out a tape recorder and notepad with a blue pen, smiling, always one for getting the last laugh.

***

Mayabeque, Cuba

PYT was in the backyard near the pool, sword dancing and meditating. She had to take a shower and get ready to meet with Juda and Costilla dealing with oil prices. She had her hands in so much oil she didn't even need to sell drugs.

PYT had been exercising for two hours now and she was a little drained. She checked her Rolex bust down watch to see if she had time for a nap. As soon as she turned to leave, she felt someone behind her making her stop.

"You still slow, Zeema," her sister Za'alya said, standing twenty feet behind her in a black catsuit with a long sword in her hand.

PYT turned around with rage, looking at her sister, who looked like she lost twenty-five pounds or more.

"You killed my husband."

"Yes, but whoever that crazy Spanish bitch was, I'ma be sure to kill her too. She grazed me. But first I'ma kill you," Za'alya said, smiling

PYT had no clue who she was talking about but right now that didn't matter at all.

"You talking too much, bitch," PYT said as she ran towards her with her sword in the air.

The women went back to back in a vicious sword fight

Za'alya ducked as PYT swung the sword at her head, almost taking it off. PYT was in full force as Za'alya did two flips backpedaling, catching her breath.

"I'ma kill you," Za'alya gritted, rushing PYT, swinging her sword left to right at the speed of lightning, slicing her in her lower abdomen as she clutched it in pain.

PYT went sword for sword with her sister as sparks were flying in the air like in the *300* movies.

Both women grew tired. Sweat was pouring down both of their foreheads, but that didn't stop the fight.

PYT kicked Za'alya in the chest and cut her in the face, taking out a big piece of chunk.

Za'alya grabbed her right side of her face to see her hand quickly covered in blood.

"You bitch!" Za'alya shouted, feeling as if half her face came off.

PYT smiled and continued to go to work. Her sister was blocking every hit, but what she did next was very skillful.

Za'alya dropped low in a split and stabbed PYT in her right leg then hopped up and kicked her in her face, dropping her. Now Za'alya was standing over her with her sword at PYT's neck.

"Got you now. Bye bye."

As soon as Za'alya was about to stab her in the neck, a bullet hit her in her shoulder, then bullets started coming back to back, making her run.

PYT didn't know who was shooting. She hid next to a wheelbarrow as she saw Za'alya was long gone through the woods.

Seconds later, the guards came running out back. When PYT exercised they would normally take a break because she wanted nobody around.

"Who was that shooting?" She asked the fourteen guards now checking to see if she was okay, because she looked hurt and was soaked in blood.

"I don't know, boss. The only person who was here was Savannah seconds ago," one of them said in Spanish.

PYT forgot Savannah was even around because she didn't even see her or speak to her. She wondered why she just saved her life. As she limped back to the house, she remembered what Za'alya said about a Spanish woman who shot her after killing Rugar. Her mind went to Savannah, then back to Za'alya. She had so much going on she forgot Za'alya was still out there.

The house nurse cleaned all her cuts and bandaged her up then gave her some meds to take the pain away.

Romell Tukes

Chapter 32
Palm Beach, FL

Romell was in his beach condo staring out the windows thinking it had been four months since he was a wanted man. He was planning to fly out the state again to Romania to lay low, but he didn't want to leave everything just yet. He still had a lot of shit going on. Now with a son by Katie, he had more shit to worry about.

An hour ago he was on the phone with Naya talking about future plans for their family if anything was to go wrong. Never would he believe a nigga he grew up with in the sandbox would give him up to the feds. When he got wind of Southside snitching, he was crushed, but number one rule to the streets never snitch. So when he heard Southside broke the code on him, he had to treat him like he never knew him and put a tag on his head. His little man killed Southside and was blessed with so much money he could make every commissary with his life bid.

Romell heard keys and knew it was Naya. She was the only one who got keys to this private condo. He called her name and heard nothing.

He walked into the living room only to be tackled by two huge white boys with FBI uniforms on. Sixteen others surrounded him with their rifles drawn.

"We got you now, you bastard," the agents said while cuffing him up.

Once he was read his rights he was led into a van and taken into custody. All he could think about was the son he only saw one time in the UK. He wished he would have stayed.

***

Romell was now back in Miami at the FBI headquarters in a room with an agent he never saw. He was waiting on his two lawyers to arrive, both females.

"So as you know, you're considered a kingpin and you're facing a lot of time, but where there is a will, there is a way my mother used to always say," the big muscle head white man stated in a tight FBI shirt and pants.

"Fuck your mother! Now give me my fucking lawyer call," he stated sharply.

The agent chuckled. Normally he would have beat the shit out of a criminal for talking crazy, but Romell was a very dangerous man with major connections.

"Okay tough guy. You must be cut from a different cloth. It's no need for us to let you call your lawyers because they are already downstairs, I believe," he said, getting up, ice grilling Romell as he walked out.

After talking to his lawyers for an hour, they agreed to try to set a bail hearing so he could get out on bill.

Once the lawyers left, they placed him in a holding cell with two other men he never saw, both Cuban.

They charged him with thirty-seven counts of all types of crazy serious charges. All he could think about was his family.

This was the part of the game he hated. This was the part rappers ain't never talk about in their songs. This was the part of the game that made niggas lose their hair and look 40 at 20 years old.

***

New York City

It was a windy cold night in the city, but everybody was out because it was the night of Super Bowl.

Agent Berkeley and Captain Raymond were both enjoying the football game at the sports bar and their favorite football team was playing.

"I think I'll retire soon. I'm sick of the headache. I'm on my third wife since I've been with the Bureau," Captain Raymond said, drinking Jack Daniels liquor.

"Yeah, I'm just starting. This is the biggest bust of my whole career. Who would ever think some low life gangbangers would turn into the biggest kingpin on the east coast connected to some powerful people?" Agent Berkeley stated, sitting on the stool of the packed bar as people yelled and shouted.

"It's time for me to go," Raymond said, feeling wasted as if he had too much.

"Yeah, me too," Berkeley said, watching his team lose.

"Please, my team losing. I should have been left this cigar smoking shit hole."

"I got work early anyway, and I know my wife waiting on me," said Berkeley

"I know the vibes."

"Trust me, you don't. I got caught fucking her porn star sister last month, so I really been in dog shit," he said paying the bills as Raymond looked at him as if he was nuts.

"How was it? I never fucked a porn star," Raymond wondered as they walked out of the bar to their car.

"Bro, she is a beautiful girl, but she had no walls, nothing. It felt like gorilla pussy and her pussy lips looked like liver meat hanging off a stick," he said as they both laughed.

There were so many cars in the small parking lot they couldn't find theirs. They knew they would have a hard time getting out since everybody was bumper to bumper.

"There we go. Your car next to mines," Raymond said, pointing at his Lincoln Town Car in the back.

Before they made it to the back, shots were coming there direction from the front, backs, and sides.

Raymond got hit two times in his chest, but he was still able to pull out and shoot back, hitting one of the gunmen in the face.

Berkeley took cover, shooting back while trying to call for backup on the walkie talkie he always carried.

The gunmen were closing in on them. Three of them split up and ambushed both agents. Berkeley saw he was closed in and he was out of bullets. The two killers aired him out, leaving him dead under a car tire.

Raymond jumped up from a bike, hitting both of the killers, but forgetting there was one man left as sirens could be heard.

"Goodnight," Bullet said as he blew Raymond's brains out.

Bullet took off into the night as if he was a ninja of some type.

Chapter 33
Miami, FL

Naya was sitting on her bathroom toilet nodding off, trying to stay awake. Luckily Brandon was at his martial art practice so that gave her some time to get herself together.

She grabbed the glass mirror off the sink and sniffed one of the six lines of tannish-brown substance.

It had been months since Romell's arrest and his trial was supposed to start next month, she felt as if her life was snatched from under her. She even stopped praying and stopped going to Jumah because her mind wasn't clear. The only thing she could do to numb her pain was sniff dope. She was scared of needles so shooting it was out of the picture for her.

When she picked up this habit months ago she was just experimenting until she got hooked on heroin. Now she was normally high all day to cope with life. She hoped her son would never find out.

Naya took another hit so strong she had to lean her head back as she felt her body get a warm sensual feeling.

"You went from a boss to a junkie. Damn, you can thank me later for what I'm about to do," a female voice stated slowly as Naya thought she was daydreaming

"Uhhh..." Naya mumbled as she slowly opened her colorful eyes to see a woman standing there with a gun pointed at her.

Naya was so fucked up on cloud nine she didn't even hear her come in. She didn't even know how she got past the four guards patrolling the front of the large mansion Romell left her.

"Where is Zeema?"

"I don't know. You tell me," Naya said with a slurred high voice, knowing today she would meet her maker.

"I only ask once, but since you're my half-sister, I'ma ask you again. Where is she?" Za'alya asked, now frustrated. Seeing how high Naya was made her lose so much respect for her.

It was easy finding Naya and killing her guards was easy, she just acted as if she was a jogger new to the area as she approached the mansion gates. She killed all four of them then entered the beautiful home on one mission.

"Just kill me, bitch. I have nothing to live for anyway!" Naya shouted with tears.

"Yeah, that sounds like my life. And I hate them eyes," Za'alya said.

Bloc, Bloc, Bloc!

Naya was in shock when she saw Za'alya's body fall on the sink, shattering the glass mirror as the dope flew everywhere.

"You okay, Mom?" Brandon asked with a smoking gun in his hand looking in his mom's eyes to see she was high again but trying to sober up.

"Yes," she said, seeing no remorse in his eyes for what he had just done.

"Go get yourself together. Me and the guards are going to clean this up," Brandon said, sounding like a true killer at only fourteen years old.

"Okay," she said, upset and disappointed in herself for letting her son catch her like this. There was no doubt in her mind that he didn't know what she was doing.

She left the room as three guards walked in the bathroom with their guns out to see Brandon standing there, which shocked them.

"Clean this shit up," he said before walking out to go check on his mom.

***

Compton, LA

Bullet was on the West Coast at one of his six baby mother's cribs, tearing her ass up. He had her on all fours.

"Ugghhh, fuck this phat ass!" Candy shouted as she forced her ass back on his dick as he slid his thumb in her asshole, making her go crazy.

They had been fucking for forty minutes straight. Their daughter was in the next room sleeping hard.

There was a loud boom as if the door was kicked off the frame, which made both of them jump out of the bed naked. Before he could even get his clothes on, agents rushed in his room which was dark with red beams on their assault rifles.

"Freeze…FBI…don't move!"

"I ain't do shit!" Candy yelled.

"Shut the fuck up. You're both under arrest. Take them in!" one of the agents yelled.

"Please, my daughter is next door!" Candy yelled, leaving the house in cuffs.

"She'll be okay in foster care. I grew up in the system," one of them said, laughing.

Bullet spit in two of their faces before they started stomping a mud hole in his face.

***

LA County Jail

Bullet was in the bullpen with 100 Crips and twenty West Coast Piru Bloods all on mainline ready to bang for their hood when they got upstairs.

Bullet told the Feds he had nothing to talk about. He thought he was being arrested for the federal indictment against the Empire. Once they told him his new charges of killing two federal agents he was sick, but he was past sick when he saw the video of him killing the two out back of the sports bar in New York six months ago.

His baby mother was charged with money laundering and bank fraud.

Bullet let it be known off the rip he was an East Coast Blood and he was with whatever. He was a big nigga, so they thought against trying shit.

Bullet called his lawyer and told him what happened and he told him he should be getting shipped back to New York soon.

Chapter 34
Newburg, NY
Months later

PYT was driving in an all-black Cadillac CTS up the 9A route towards a small town outside of Newburg called Coldspring. Today she was alone and on a mission. Lately her life had been filled with drama, death, and pain.

Since China took over the Cartel Commission, things got bad. She had been raising the prices on the pills, coke, and oil. Nobody could do anything about it, not even PYT, but a lot of families wanted her out. She was using her power to the extreme. She was getting a lot of powerful people hit in Cuba in position so she could control everything. China was power stuck, PYT tried to talk to her, but it was useless.

Since Rugar's death she had been having crazy nightmares but she was somewhat happy his killer was now dead. When Naya told PYT how Za'alya caught her slipping, leaving out the drug part, she wasn't surprised when she heard Brandon killed her sister. PYT wanted to save her sister for last, but she knew her days were numbered regardless.

It was dark out as PYT pulled up to the quiet suburban middle class neighborhood with nice houses and clean cut grass. She was looking for number 4172 and finally found it at the end of the block. It was a yellow brick house with two vans in the small driveway. This was where Twin was being held in a witness protection program guarded by agents 24/7.

He was placed here until after the Empire trial. Since Red Hat disappeared the same day he was blocked in on the bridge, Bullet was the leader of the now eighty-six man indictment.

Without Twin being the main witness, the government didn't have a lot of evidence to go off of besides Bullet killing Raymond on camera.

She was still a part of the Empire. She was just smart enough not to get caught up, plus she was their plug, so she had to move smarter, even though she had agents on the payroll.

PYT hopped out with her mask and gloves on, ready to handle her business.

***

Twin was in his room playing XBOX while smoking a blunt of sour diesel. Twin planned to take the stand next month and tell it all. He only felt bad if he was to say anything about Naya because she was still like a sister to him, so he planned to keep her name out of it.

To be honest, he didn't give a fuck about Red Hat, PYT, Rugar, Bullet, or Big Smokey. He was a Jersey boy and they were from New York. He would never tell on anybody from Jersey. He still consider himself a real nigga. He knew a lot of niggas who ratted and came home and were still that guy on the street.

After trial, he made a deal to go down south to North Caroline to sell bricks and set niggas up for the Feds. He was happy to be free, still be in the field, live life, and get money while the real niggas sat down for a long time - as long as it wasn't him.

Twin heard noises as if the guards were doing jumping jacks or some type of jumping. His room was right next to the living room, where four guards were at all times.

As soon as he stepped foot out his door in his basketball shorts and tank top, he froze, wishing he would have stayed in the room or in jail.

"You really thought you was going to get away with this shit, rat nigga?" PYT said, walking over four dead bodies of federal agents.

"PYT, I'm sorry. I had no choice. I didn't tell on you," he said, lying, seeing the long silencer on the barrel of her gun

"It don't matter. You told period, nigga. Ain't no rules or levels to snitching," PYT said, seeing the look in his eyes as if he was ready to do something.

"But..." he said, stuttering, reaching for one of the dead agent's gun on the desk a half of a foot away from him.

PYT emptied the clip in him, then walked out shaking her head, knowing the game was fucked up.

***

Jacksonville, FL

Shah of the India Cartel was in a rush as she walked down the back alley of a friend's hair store with six big goons.

She opened the steel door and walked down the dark stairs to see her guards surrounding the woman she had been hunting for so long she gave up.

Shah hated coming to America for anything. She had very little connections in the States, but the ones she did just helped her find her daughter.

Shah looked at the young woman and tears flooded her eyes because it was her. She could tell by the eyes that only she, PYT, Naya and the young woman sitting in a chair in front of her had now.

"Who are you?" the woman said, pissed off. She was just kidnapped and teased and brought here.

Shah saw her black garment and hijab. She was her father's daughter. He was a powerful Arabian Muslim man in the Middle East.

"I'm your mother," Shah said, now face to face.

"You have a mistake. I'm——" Hosayni paused when she saw the woman's eyes remembering those same eyes when she was a baby.

"It's okay. I'm here for you," Shah said, hugging her.

"Why, why did you leave? They killed my father and sold me into sex trafficking," Hosayni said, crying.

"I had to do the same thing with your older sisters but I'm back in your lives now. The past is the past," she said wiping her daughter's tears.

"Sister?" she asked, confused.

"Yes, PYT and Naya, who also live in the States."

When Shah said this she saw her daughter gave her an evil, deadly look.

"It can't be."

"You heard of them?" Shah asked.

"I'm going to kill them both. They killed everything I loved," Hosayni said, emotional.

"Those are your sisters. I'm sure we can all talk this out. Come on, I'm taking you home," Shah stated.

"To where?"

"India." Shah left with her daughter, seeing how broken down she looked with bags under her eyes and dirty fingernails.

They all left with clouded minds.

Chapter 35
Miami, FL

Naya and China were having a girls' night at Naya's mansion while Brandon was spending the weekend at a friend's house.

China was normally in Cuba, but she needed some time to get away from her busy life, not to mention the next cartel meeting was a couple of months away.

Both women sat on the couch in the large high ceilinged living room watching the 52" inch flat screen TV and drinking wine, enjoying each other's company.

"Damn, girl, I can't believe how fast my life changed. I remember when I was in high school working in your store," China said, sitting Indian style on the couch.

"Yeah, you were the best worker, and you never stole like them little hoodrats who I always used to catch on camera stealing out the cash register," Naya said. She was feeling nice, but she was ready to take another hit of smack she had in her bathroom cabinet.

"I have to be real. I was stealing from time to time."

"China, no you weren't!" Naya yelled, shocked, with a chuckle.

"Yeah, I'm sorry, girl. Times were hard back then living off of Under Pond. Rugar was like signing an IOU agreement. But Brazy did everything for me," China said, thinking about her brother Brazy. She loved him to death.

"Yeah, I never met nobody like him. His heart was made of gold and diamonds," Naya stated. She sipped some more wine out of her glass while playing with the rim of the glass with her manicured nails.

Naya missed Brazy every day. If it wasn't for him, she would have been a regular hoodrat with a pretty face and nice

body. He showed her what a woman was really about and how she should carry herself and how to let other people carry her.

She knew if he was alive, she wouldn't be sniffing heroin or taking opium pills. He would have killed her himself.

"Where is your bathroom?"

"Down the hall to your far left," Naya said as she watched TV, something she rarely had time to do.

"A'ight," China said as she got up with her big ass sitting in her white Gucci jeans.

China went in the bathroom to see it was spotlessly clean. She looked in the cabinet to see a bottle which was supposed to be used for pills, but instead it had a brown powder substance. China smiled, but it was a wicked smile. She found what she was looking for: dope.

"Jackpot," China mumbled as she reached in her Gucci purse to pull out a small clear glass bottle filled with rat poison in a powder form. China dumped the poison in the pill bottle and shook it up while smiling as if she was doing a good deed, but she knew Naya was getting high a week ago.

"Payback's a bitch. You think I don't know you set my brother up and helped break my family apart?" China said out loud as if she was talking to friends.

China always thought Naya was the reason why Brazy was dead and her family was the way it was now.

She flushed the toilet and washed her hands as if she had really used the bathroom, then made her way back to the living room.

"Naya, I got to get going. I have to catch this flight back to Cuba. But I love you, gurl. Take care of yourself," China said, hugging her and then rushing out to where her guards were waiting on her in two Yukon trucks.

"Okay, see you later," Naya said, walking her out, happy she could go and take a hit.

Without even locking the door, she rushed to the bathroom cabinets. Once she found what she was looking for in her pill bottle, she grabbed her pocket-size mirror from under the sink and took a big hit.

The hit went straight to her head. Naya felt her body lock up and she started to shake before she fell on the floor.

Foam was pouring out of her mouth as her body went into shock for ninety seconds before her pulse gave out.

Naya died with her eyes wide open. By the time her guards went to check on her, she was gone.

***

Weeks Later
Dade County Jail

Romell was in his cell going through it. His trial date was next week. He found out his wife overdosed weeks ago, which was word to him because he never knew Naya for doing drugs.

He had so much on his plate. He wanted to end it all, but he couldn't. He was a fighter.

Katie came down to see him last week with his son, which was cool. She was willing to give him a chance to know his now nine-year-old son. He stared at his ceiling, thinking about life and what Allah had planned for him next.

Romell Tukes

Chapter 36
Cuba

PYT was upstairs putting on the last little touches of her makeup. She looked beautiful in her gold Celine dress with her long hair done nicely in curls. She was in her bedroom thinking about today's meeting and what would happen because a lot of the families wanted China, even if it was by death.

There was too much going on. She just buried Naya last month after an overdose. Now she felt as if she lost everybody in her life. If this was the price of power and money, then she didn't want it at all. Bullet and Romell were both facing life sentences. Romell's court date was delayed until next month while Bullet was in MDC Brooklyn awaiting trial.

Red Hat was nowhere to be found. PYT heard he jumped off a bridge, but his body was never found. One thing many didn't know about Red Hat was he was a track star and one of the best swimmers of his time.

Brandon was now living with her because he had no parents or family except her since Rugar and Naya were dead. She planned to do her best to raise him correctly. He had been through a lot in his life already. She was homeschooling him and teaching him different languages. Eight hours of his day was studying and four was focused on training.

The families were all starting to arrive and making their way towards the backyard where the meeting would be held.

As soon as she was done getting ready, there was a soft knock at the door.

"Come in!" PYT yelled.

China walked in wearing jeans and a shirt made by Prada and some heels.

"Hey, you look nice," China said, looking her up and down with her chinky eyes.

"Nah, this ain't nothing. You ready for today?"

"Of course."

"Please keep your cool, because you're not the most likeable person in the world right now," PYT said, checking her careless attitude.

"Shit, people hated Malcom X and Donald Trump, but look at everything they did for the people," China said wisely, walking around her room.

"Okay whatever. But how come you weren't at Naya's funeral? I thought you were in Florida," PYT said, fixing her hair in the mirror.

"I was busy, and she was a fucking junkie," China said, which made PYT stop what she was doing

"Look, China, I'm not going just let you talk about my sister like that," PYT said. China had her back turned to her.

"Fuck you and your sister!" China spit as she pulled out a 50 cal from her Birkin bag, aiming at PYT.

"What has gotten into you?" PYT said, seeing a crazy look in China's eyes

"You, your sister, your whole fucking family fucked my life up," China said with tears.

"China, death is a part of the game," PYT said wondering if she should try her hand and bust a move.

"Oh yeah? Well, we about even. I killed Naya, and now you."

"You what?" PYT said, filled with rage.

"Yesss, bitch, get mad," China said, laughing. "I put rat poison in her dope. But thank me later for that," China said with a wicked smile.

"You better kill me now."

"Oh, I will. Then I got a Cartel to run," China said as she pulled the trigger.

Then she was shot in the head eight times before her body dropped.

PYT was shocked. She didn't even know where the shots came from until she saw Brandon standing there with tears with a gun in his hand. His room was connected to PYT's room, so he heard everything China said about killing his mom. He had to make a choice: either to kill his mom's killer, or let his aunt live.

"It's okay," she said, hugging him, looking at China's dead body, thinking how good of a shot that was. Luckily China missed her first and only shot, or she would have been a goner.

"I know. You can go to your meeting. All the people out there waiting on you," he said without a blink of an eye.

She really loved this little nigga. He was a young don.

"Excuse me, Jasmine," a female voice said, standing at the door, causing PYT and Brandon to look.

PYT saw Shah standing there with another woman. The last time she saw her mom was at Naya's funeral, but the woman looked a little familiar.

"Hey…"

"Wrong time," Shah said, looking at China's dead body, knowing it was going to happen sooner or later. "Brandon, are you okay?" Shah asked her grandson. He nodded his head

"Who's this, Mom?" PYT asked as Hosayni stared at her oddly.

"This is your sister Hosayni, and today she will be taking my seat within the Cartel Commission because I'm retiring," Shah said.

PYT and Hosayni looked at each other.

"Okay, nice to finally meet you. I'm sure we have a lot to catch up on," PYT said as Brandon went back to his room.

"Let's go to this meeting, then after, I'll let the two of you talk," Shah said, walking out as both women followed her.

***

Everybody was sitting there wondering why China, PYT, and Shah were so late

"Hey, I'm sorry I'm late," PYT said, rushing to the table.

Shah took her seat and Hosayni stood off to the side near the pool.

"Where is the devil?" Katie said, joking.

"She is upstairs dead. She just tried to kill me and my nephew killed her, so she violated many rules," PYT said as every family member shouted with cheers.

"I was going to kill her myself," Judah said, faking scared of his own shadow.

"We also have someone retiring, and her replacement is her daughter. Ms. Shah from the Shah Cartel's other daughter will take her place today. As we all know, she is my mom, and if you didn't know, now you know," PYT said sounding like Biggie as Hosayni walked up to her mom. "Does anybody reject or go against my mother?" PYT asked.

Nobody said a word. The quiet woman did her part for years within the commission, so they respected her honor.

Hosayni then took Shah's seat as Shah stood to leave, walking out front, passing a woman.

"Welcome to the family," PYT said. "We also have a new position, which I will have to fill as the head of commission," PYT said.

"Wait!" a voice said.

Everybody saw a Spanish woman in a dress and heels walking towards their table.

When PYT saw Savannah, she got pissed because she was out of place and was up to no good.

"Who the fuck are you?" Katie asked in a rude manner; asking the million dollar question.

"I'm Hagar's daughter Savannah and I'm here to inform you all that PYT killed my mother and she violated every rule. I believe the head of the commission should be me, since I'm the next kin of blood."

PYT pulled out a gun and aimed it at Savannah while everybody else pulled out a gun as well. Most were aimed at PYT and some were aimed at Savannah. Even Hosayni had her gun pointed at PYT as she smiled...

To Be Continued...
Gangland Cartel 4
Coming Soon

Submission Guideline

Submit the first three chapters of your completed manuscript to ldpsubmissions@gmail.com, subject line: Your book's title. The manuscript must be in a .doc file and sent as an attachment. Document should be in Times New Roman, double spaced and in size 12 font. Also, provide your synopsis and full contact information. If sending multiple submissions, they must each be in a separate email.

Have a story but no way to send it electronically? You can still submit to LDP/Ca$h Presents. Send in the first three chapters, written or typed, of your completed manuscript to:

LDP: Submissions Dept
Po Box 944
Stockbridge, Ga 30281

DO NOT send original manuscript. Must be a duplicate.

Provide your synopsis and a cover letter containing your full contact information.

Thanks for considering LDP and Ca$h Presents.

Coming Soon from Lock Down Publications/Ca$h Presents

BOW DOWN TO MY GANGSTA

By **Ca$h**

TORN BETWEEN TWO

By **Coffee**

THE STREETS STAINED MY SOUL **II**

By **Marcellus Allen**

BLOOD OF A BOSS **VI**

SHADOWS OF THE GAME II

By **Askari**

LOYAL TO THE GAME **IV**

By **T.J. & Jelissa**

IF LOVING YOU IS WRONG… **III**

By **Jelissa**

TRUE SAVAGE **VIII**

MIDNIGHT CARTEL IV

DOPE BOY MAGIC IV

CITY OF KINGZ II

By **Chris Green**

BLAST FOR ME **III**

A SAVAGE DOPEBOY III

CUTTHROAT MAFIA III

DUFFLE BAG CARTEL VI

HEARTLESS GOON VI

By **Ghost**

A HUSTLER'S DECEIT III

KILL ZONE **II**

BAE BELONGS TO ME III

A DOPE BOY'S QUEEN III

By **Aryanna**

COKE KINGS V

KING OF THE TRAP II

By **T.J. Edwards**

GORILLAZ IN THE BAY V

3X KRAZY III

De'Kari

THE STREETS ARE CALLING II

Duquie Wilson

KINGPIN KILLAZ IV

STREET KINGS III

PAID IN BLOOD III

CARTEL KILLAZ IV

DOPE GODS III

Hood Rich

SINS OF A HUSTLA II

ASAD

KINGZ OF THE GAME VI

Playa Ray

SLAUGHTER GANG IV

RUTHLESS HEART IV

By Willie Slaughter

THE HEART OF A SAVAGE III

By Jibril Williams

FUK SHYT II

By Blakk Diamond

TRAP QUEEN

By Troublesome

YAYO V

GHOST MOB II

Stilloan Robinson

KINGPIN DREAMS III

By Paper Boi Rari

CREAM II

By Yolanda Moore

SON OF A DOPE FIEND III

By Renta

FOREVER GANGSTA II

GLOCKS ON SATIN SHEETS III

By Adrian Dulan

LOYALTY AIN'T PROMISED III

By Keith Williams

THE PRICE YOU PAY FOR LOVE III

By Destiny Skai

I'M NOTHING WITHOUT HIS LOVE II

SINS OF A THUG II

By Monet Dragun

LIFE OF A SAVAGE IV

MURDA SEASON IV

GANGLAND CARTEL IV

CHI'RAQ GANGSTAS III

By **Romell Tukes**

QUIET MONEY IV

EXTENDED CLIP II

By **Trai'Quan**

THE STREETS MADE ME III

By **Larry D. Wright**

IF YOU CROSS ME ONCE II

ANGEL III

By **Anthony Fields**

FRIEND OR FOE III

By **Mimi**

SAVAGE STORMS III

By **Meesha**

BLOOD ON THE MONEY III

By **J-Blunt**

THE STREETS WILL NEVER CLOSE II

By **K'ajji**

NIGHTMARES OF A HUSTLA III

By **King Dream**

THE WIFEY I USED TO BE II

By **Nicole Goosby**

IN THE ARM OF HIS BOSS

By **Jamila**

MONEY, MURDER & MEMORIES II

Malik D. Rice

CONCRETE KILLAZ II

By **Kingpen**

HARD AND RUTHLESS II

By Von Wiley Hall

LEVELS TO THIS SHYT II

By Ah'Million

MOB TIES II

By SayNoMore

BODYMORE MURDERLAND II

By Delmont Player

Available Now

RESTRAINING ORDER **I & II**

By **CA$H & Coffee**

LOVE KNOWS NO BOUNDARIES **I II & III**

By **Coffee**

RAISED AS A GOON I, II, III & IV

BRED BY THE SLUMS I, II, III

BLAST FOR ME I & II

ROTTEN TO THE CORE I II III

A BRONX TALE I, II, III

DUFFLE BAG CARTEL I II III IV V

HEARTLESS GOON I II III IV V

A SAVAGE DOPEBOY I II

DRUG LORDS I II III

CUTTHROAT MAFIA I II

By **Ghost**

LAY IT DOWN **I & II**

LAST OF A DYING BREED I II

BLOOD STAINS OF A SHOTTA I & II III

By **Jamaica**

LOYAL TO THE GAME I II III

LIFE OF SIN I, II III

By **TJ & Jelissa**

BLOODY COMMAS I & II

SKI MASK CARTEL I II & III

KING OF NEW YORK I II,III IV V

RISE TO POWER I II III

COKE KINGS I II III IV

BORN HEARTLESS I II III IV

KING OF THE TRAP

By **T.J. Edwards**

IF LOVING HIM IS WRONG...I & II

LOVE ME EVEN WHEN IT HURTS I II III

By **Jelissa**

WHEN THE STREETS CLAP BACK I & II III

THE HEART OF A SAVAGE I II

By **Jibril Williams**

A DISTINGUISHED THUG STOLE MY HEART I II & III

LOVE SHOULDN'T HURT I II III IV

RENEGADE BOYS I II III IV

PAID IN KARMA I II III

SAVAGE STORMS I II

Gangland Cartel 3

By **Meesha**
A GANGSTER'S CODE I &, II III
A GANGSTER'S SYN I II III
THE SAVAGE LIFE I II III
CHAINED TO THE STREETS I II III
BLOOD ON THE MONEY I II
By J-Blunt
PUSH IT TO THE LIMIT
By **Bre' Hayes**
BLOOD OF A BOSS **I, II, III, IV, V**
SHADOWS OF THE GAME
By **Askari**
THE STREETS BLEED MURDER **I, II & III**
THE HEART OF A GANGSTA I II& III
By **Jerry Jackson**
CUM FOR ME I II III IV V VI
An **LDP Erotica Collaboration**
BRIDE OF A HUSTLA **I II & II**
THE FETTI GIRLS **I, II& III**
CORRUPTED BY A GANGSTA I, II III, IV
BLINDED BY HIS LOVE
THE PRICE YOU PAY FOR LOVE I II
DOPE GIRL MAGIC I II III
By **Destiny Skai**
WHEN A GOOD GIRL GOES BAD
By **Adrienne**
THE COST OF LOYALTY I II III

By Kweli

A GANGSTER'S REVENGE **I II III & IV**

THE BOSS MAN'S DAUGHTERS I II III IV V

A SAVAGE LOVE **I & II**

BAE BELONGS TO ME I II

A HUSTLER'S DECEIT I, II, III

WHAT BAD BITCHES DO I, II, III

SOUL OF A MONSTER I II III

KILL ZONE

A DOPE BOY'S QUEEN I II

By **Aryanna**

A KINGPIN'S AMBITON

A KINGPIN'S AMBITION **II**

I MURDER FOR THE DOUGH

By **Ambitious**

TRUE SAVAGE I II III IV V VI VII

DOPE BOY MAGIC I, II, III

MIDNIGHT CARTEL I II III

CITY OF KINGZ

By **Chris Green**

A DOPEBOY'S PRAYER

By **Eddie "Wolf" Lee**

THE KING CARTEL **I, II & III**

By **Frank Gresham**

THESE NIGGAS AIN'T LOYAL **I, II & III**

By **Nikki Tee**

GANGSTA SHYT **I II &III**

By **CATO**

THE ULTIMATE BETRAYAL

By **Phoenix**

BOSS'N UP **I , II & III**

By **Royal Nicole**

I LOVE YOU TO DEATH

By Destiny J

I RIDE FOR MY HITTA

I STILL RIDE FOR MY HITTA

By **Misty Holt**

LOVE & CHASIN' PAPER

By **Qay Crockett**

TO DIE IN VAIN

SINS OF A HUSTLA

By **ASAD**

BROOKLYN HUSTLAZ

By **Boogsy Morina**

BROOKLYN ON LOCK I & II

By **Sonovia**

GANGSTA CITY

By **Teddy Duke**

A DRUG KING AND HIS DIAMOND I & II III

A DOPEMAN'S RICHES

HER MAN, MINE'S TOO I, II

CASH MONEY HO'S

THE WIFEY I USED TO BE

By Nicole Goosby

TRAPHOUSE KING **I II & III**
KINGPIN KILLAZ I II III
STREET KINGS I II
PAID IN BLOOD **I II**
CARTEL KILLAZ I II III
DOPE GODS I II
By **Hood Rich**
LIPSTICK KILLAH **I, II, III**
CRIME OF PASSION I II & III
FRIEND OR FOE I II
By **Mimi**
STEADY MOBBN' **I, II, III**
THE STREETS STAINED MY SOUL
By **Marcellus Allen**
WHO SHOT YA **I, II, III**
SON OF A DOPE FIEND I II
Renta
GORILLAZ IN THE BAY **I II III IV**
TEARS OF A GANGSTA I II
3X KRAZY I II
DE'KARI
TRIGGADALE I II III
Elijah R. Freeman
GOD BLESS THE TRAPPERS I, II, III
THESE SCANDALOUS STREETS I, II, III
FEAR MY GANGSTA I, II, III IV, V
THESE STREETS DON'T LOVE NOBODY I, II

BURY ME A G I, II, III, IV, V

A GANGSTA'S EMPIRE I, II, III, IV

THE DOPEMAN'S BODYGAURD I II

THE REALEST KILLAZ I II III

Tranay Adams

THE STREETS ARE CALLING

Duquie Wilson

MARRIED TO A BOSS... I II III

By Destiny Skai & Chris Green

KINGZ OF THE GAME I II III IV V

Playa Ray

SLAUGHTER GANG I II III

RUTHLESS HEART I II III

By Willie Slaughter

FUK SHYT

By Blakk Diamond

DON'T F#CK WITH MY HEART I II

By Linnea

ADDICTED TO THE DRAMA I II III

IN THE ARM OF HIS BOSS II

By Jamila

YAYO I II III IV

A SHOOTER'S AMBITION I II

By S. Allen

TRAP GOD I II III

By Troublesome

FOREVER GANGSTA

GLOCKS ON SATIN SHEETS I II

By Adrian Dulan

TOE TAGZ I II III

LEVELS TO THIS SHYT

By Ah'Million

KINGPIN DREAMS I II

By Paper Boi Rari

CONFESSIONS OF A GANGSTA I II III

By Nicholas Lock

I'M NOTHING WITHOUT HIS LOVE

SINS OF A THUG

By Monet Dragun

CAUGHT UP IN THE LIFE I II III

By Robert Baptiste

NEW TO MONEY, MURDER & MEMORIES

THE GAME I II III

By **Malik D. Rice**

LIFE OF A SAVAGE I II III

A GANGSTA'S QUR'AN I II III

MURDA SEASON I II III

GANGLAND CARTEL I II III

CHI'RAQ GANGSTAS I II

By **Romell Tukes**

LOYALTY AIN'T PROMISED I II

By Keith Williams

QUIET MONEY I II III

THUG LIFE I II

EXTENDED CLIP

By **Trai'Quan**

THE STREETS MADE ME I II

By **Larry D. Wright**

THE ULTIMATE SACRIFICE I, II, III, IV, V, VI

KHADIFI

IF YOU CROSS ME ONCE

ANGEL I II

By **Anthony Fields**

THE LIFE OF A HOOD STAR

By **Ca$h & Rashia Wilson**

THE STREETS WILL NEVER CLOSE

By **K'ajji**

CREAM

By **Yolanda Moore**

NIGHTMARES OF A HUSTLA I II

By **King Dream**

CONCRETE KILLAZ

By **Kingpen**

HARD AND RUTHLESS

By **Von Wiley Hall**

GHOST MOB II

Stilloan Robinson

MOB TIES

By **SayNoMore**

BODYMORE MURDERLAND

By **Delmont Player**

<u>BOOKS BY LDP'S CEO, CA$H</u>

<u>TRUST IN NO MAN</u>

<u>TRUST IN NO MAN 2</u>

<u>TRUST IN NO MAN 3</u>

<u>BONDED BY BLOOD</u>

<u>SHORTY GOT A THUG</u>

<u>THUGS CRY</u>

<u>THUGS CRY 2</u>

<u>THUGS CRY 3</u>

<u>TRUST NO BITCH</u>

<u>TRUST NO BITCH 2</u>

<u>TRUST NO BITCH 3</u>

<u>TIL MY CASKET DROPS</u>

<u>RESTRAINING ORDER</u>

<u>RESTRAINING ORDER 2</u>

<u>IN LOVE WITH A CONVICT</u>

<u>LIFE OF A HOOD STAR</u>

CPSIA information can be obtained
at www.ICGtesting.com
Printed in the USA
BVHW040223291221
625121BV00013B/685